A CHRISTMAS PUPPY TO CHERISH

JOSIE RIVIERA

INTRODUCTION

To keep up on newly released ebooks, paperbacks, Large Print Paperbacks, audiobooks, as well as exclusive sales, sign up for Josie's Newsletter today.

As a thank you, I'll send you a Free PDF ... The Beauty Of ...

Josie's Newsletter

Did you know that according to a Yale University study, people who read books live longer?

PRAISE AND AWARDS

USA TODAY bestselling author

#22 Amazon Bestseller Contemporary Christian Romance

#24 Amazon Bestseller Contemporary Christian Romance Books

#29 Amazon Bestseller Religious Romance

5 STAR READER REVIEWS

"A page turning holiday read with relatable characters and unique story elements. A common theme of characters, who loved nature and animals. As an avid reader, I enjoy how Josie Riviera included Sarah adopting to her hearing loss. Also enjoyed that Max, not only was a bird watcher but was teaching budgies to talk and mimic other birds. Not too many characters play the harmonica. So grab a cup of hot chocolate and a warm blanket and enjoy this delightful Christmas romance." - Amazon Reviewer

"A nice combination of characters....Max, Sarah and also the message of Christmas. Loving nature, the environment was perfect with the birds and the others of the forest. Toss in a harmonica and a puppy....(who doesn't love a little puppy?).and the scene is set. Truly a wonderful positive story for this upcoming season. Most highly recommended..." - Amazon Reviewer

"A sweet story with very likable characters. Who can resist a woman who takes in strays and arranges flowers. Certainly not a bird researcher who accepts her guidance. Even though she has hearing loss and he enjoys listening to birds, their love of nature brings them together. But when his research ends she wonders if she will see him again." - Amazon Reviewer

CHAPTER ONE

*M*axwell Archer gave up. The harmonica wasn't there.

He might as well walk the short distance from his rental home in Cherish, South Carolina, to Musically Yours, the local music store. The store was reputed to be the finest in town. Likewise, it was also the only music store in the small town.

Open suitcases lay on the floor in the compact, plain living room of his rental. Further cluttering the room was a confusion of chirping budgies, oversized birdcages, and a stack of research notes piled beside his computer. He definitely needed some air.

Momentarily diverted by Angel, a silvery green budgie who chattered, "God bless us, every one," over and over, Max shrugged on his olive-green twill jacket, uttered a brief good-bye, and headed out the door.

He'd recited numerous words to his parakeets. The key to teaching a parakeet to talk was repetition, but "God bless us, every one," was the only phrase Angel repeated. She was a rescue bird, and her previous owner had been an elderly woman who apparently had watched Charles Dickens's, *A Christmas Carol*, on television many times.

The other two parakeets—one timid, the other bolder—squawked, chirped, and carried on between themselves.

As Max strolled, a brisk December breeze invigorated him, and he paused to regard the poignantly familiar mom and pop shops. Whitney's, the ice cream store, and Big Brothers Big Sisters, where he'd spent many afternoons after school finishing his homework. The brick building looked the same.

At twelve years old, Max had delivered the *Sunday Sentinel* to all the businesses along Main Street, accompanied by a racing dog his foster family, the Monroes, had owned. He remembered that dog. He loved that dog. A Labrador husky named Tinsel.

He couldn't contain his smile as he reminisced.

The calendar showed December fifth, and downtown was in the process of being transformed into a Yuletide fairyland. Numerous workers scurried past him, draping tiny white lights on bushes and sprinkling artificial snow over miniature pine trees.

Through the years, he'd indulged in visions of settling here in Cherish. He had envisioned a prestigious house on the prosperous outskirts and living out his days wealthy and respected.

Three decades had passed, and he hadn't accumulated wealth in any sense of the word. In fact, his last year's research project had been stalled because of insufficient funding.

And respected? In academic circles, perhaps. He fingered the bow tie beneath his chin—his acknowledgement to the realm of academic nerds, in which he was a charter member.

In any event, his appointment to the ornithology department of a large university in Jacksonville, Florida, began January first.

As he stepped inside the music store, a slim woman with dark hair and striking green eyes greeted him.

"May I help you?" she asked.

He nodded toward the frosted-glass front window decorated with treble clef signs, animated polar bears, and a model train weaving around an ice-covered mountain scene. "Nice." He made a comical face. "The motifs enhance the window with a ..."

She raised an eyebrow. "Festive touch?"

"Complete with tiny icicles." He moved inside, toward a shelf crammed with key holders and picked up a key holder shaped like an amplifier. Clever. However, he doubted he was allowed to hammer nails into his temporary rental house.

He sighed and surveyed the tidy store. "Do you sell harmonicas?" he asked.

"Yes. A wide assortment." The woman nodded toward a side wall. "Is this for a Christmas gift?"

"For myself. I lost my harmonica during my move." He rubbed his shoulders and unzipped his jacket. Though his rental was furnished, his limbs ached from lifting heavy bird cages and suitcases. He was an academic, not a body-builder.

In addition, his brain was flooded with information. He'd been embedded in research the entire morning when he should have been unpacking. The hours flew by whenever he examined data and he frequently lost track of time.

"Any particular brand or style?" she was asking.

"Fenders. Key of C."

"I'll show you our bestseller, which comes with a vented plastic case." She wended around numerous aisles, located a gold-edged case on a display shelf, and handed it to him. "Here's our most popular model. A twenty-tone diatonic harmonica in the key of C."

"An exact replacement for the one I lost." He ran his fingers along the case. "Thanks."

A sudden, booming symphony burst through the speakers, and they both jumped.

"Sorry," the woman said. "The background music in the store constantly needs adjustment." With a self-conscious grin, she dashed to the counter and lowered the volume. "Beethoven will do that."

"Do what?

"Startle customers with crashing chords." She darted him a sideways glance. "I haven't seen you before, by the way."

Well, that didn't take long, he thought. A stranger in a small town called for questions from the local shop owner.

"I lived here for a brief spell when I attended junior high school," he said. "I arrived yesterday after an almost three-decade absence."

She didn't press for additional information, and he didn't elaborate.

"Are you here permanently?" she asked.

"Only for December. Then I'm off to my dream job in Florida." Again, he massaged his nape. Was it from the move or stress? "My name is Max, by the way. Maxwell Archer."

"Hi, Max. I'm Dorothy Edwards. My husband, Ryan, and I own this store and we sell music, instruments, and fun novelties. We also offer lessons if you're ever interested."

"Which instruments?"

"Harp, voice, guitar and piano." She hailed an entering customer with a warm smile. "Joanna, are you here for your harp lesson with Ms. Emmanuelle?"

The little girl nodded.

"She's waiting in her studio."

"Thanks. Is the puppy here? Ms. Emmanuelle mentioned that he might be."

"He's in the back."

"Yay!" The girl's face brightened. "Sorry, I'm late." She clutched her music to her chest and hurried past them.

"Joanna attends Big Brothers Big Sisters," Dorothy said. "Are you familiar with the organization?"

"Yes."

Uncertain where the conversation might be leading, Max looked away. The last subject he cared to discuss was the Big Brothers program. He remembered it well. Fond memories surfaced. Some not so fond as well, but those weren't because of the excellent program.

"Scarlett, who is married to Joseph Slater, is heavily involved," Dorothy went on. "Emmanuelle is providing Joanna with free instruction and a harp. Joseph is a well-known worship singer and songwriter. He's also on our staff when he isn't touring."

"I've never heard of him," Max said.

"Do you listen to contemporary Christian music?"

"Never." Max dismissed her inquiry with a wave. "Does anyone teach harmonica? I play for fun, not professionally, but always appreciate any tips."

"Sorry, we don't. Try YouTube," she joked.

He had. He did. On a shoe-string academic budget, self-taught lessons suited Max perfectly. Learning had little to do with musicality, and more to do with determination, goal-setting, and an appreciation for music.

Dorothy set the harmonica on the counter. "What brings you here, Max?"

"I study budgies and how they mimic birdsongs and music." He smiled and handed her his credit card.

She rang up the order. "The two are related?"

"Absolutely. To quote a noted philosopher, 'birds vocalize conventional scales.'"

"Interesting."

Interesting? The fact was more than interesting.

"You studied birds in college?" she asked.

"Yes. I earned a master's degree from a New York City university affiliated with the Audubon Society."

"Is New York City home for you?"

"I don't have a permanent home. I drove down from New York to Cherish yesterday."

"A ten-hour trip," she commiserated. "My husband travels to Atlanta for opera rehearsals, and the four hours back and forth is exhausting."

"My trip was quite an adventure—to put it mildly, especially with three parakeets, all my possessions stuffed into two suitcases and a canvas backpack." He grimaced as he recalled the harrowing journey through the icy Virginia mountains.

"The birds stayed in their cages?"

"I can't imagine them flying around my van while I drive. I secured their cages with seat belts." Max leaned forward, warming to the conversation. "For safety reasons, I always remove the mirrors, bells, and swings, and placed their wooden perches close to the bottom of their cages. And I keep bottled water handy for refilling their cups."

"Good to know." Dorothy shot him a tongue-in-cheek smile. "Not that I ever plan on purchasing a pet. My brother, Nicholas, owns Molly Belle, an overgrown pup who gets into everything. That dog cured me of owning any animals."

Max chuckled. "In some respects, birds are easier than dogs."

"Nicholas is trying to find a home for a puppy that showed up at the sheriff's station a couple days ago. Are you interested?"

"What type of dog?"

"He's guessing a mixed breed—a toy poodle and Yorkshire Terrier."

"A Yorkipoo."

"Maybe. He's a real cutie, brown with silvery-white markings." She paused. "Wait. I'll be right back."

Dorothy emerged two minutes later clasping a puppy to her chest. She set him down and the puppy bound forward in little jumps, then stuck his nose under the counter. Furiously, he tugged on a pencil that had fallen.

"No, no. He loves to chew." At the sound of Dorothy's voice, the little ball of fur rushed headlong down an aisle, apparently unheeding of her calls. He turned a corner and almost lost his balance. Dorothy scooped him up and brought him over to Max. He licked Max's outstretched fingers as he petted him.

"He's a cute pup, isn't he?" Dorothy asked.

"He's also a bundle of charming, unrestrained energy."

"Any chance—"

"Sorry." Max shook his head. "I'm only in town for a month." Plus, he'd vowed never to own a dog again. He'd missed Tinsel too much after he'd been placed with another foster family.

Dorothy returned the puppy to the back room, then placed Max's harmonica and a complimentary candy cane in a bag. "I'm sorry it's such a short stay, but this town is welcoming, especially during the Christmas season."

Max expected he'd enjoy spending December in Cherish. The lease on his apartment in New York had ended, and he'd preferred to travel in early December rather than January.

"Are you a musician?" she asked, offering an irrepressible grin. "Naturally you are—considering you're in a music store purchasing a harmonica. Ryan and I are—"

"Concert artists."

She handed the bag to him. "I'm a pianist."

"And Ryan is an opera singer."

She tipped her head. "How did you know?"

"My friend Gerry Adams lives in Perrytown. He often shops in your store."

Unlike many of the undergraduate students Max taught his online Joy of Birdwatching classes to, Gerry had been interested and engaged. Most of Max's students selected his course as an easy elective.

Not Gerry. In his fifties, he'd developed an increasing appreciation for Max's expertise that had led to a friendly rapport between the two men. Gerry had become a sort of guru, offering guidance and awareness on another subject that interested Max: music.

"I know him." A smile dawned on Dorothy's face. "Gerry sings in the choir at Memorial Street Church."

No comment on the church part, though Max had recognized the wooden sign mounted above the store's entrance.

Proverbs 19:21.

He once knew the proverb, but could no longer recall the words.

Dorothy cast her gaze heavenward. "'Many are the plans in a person's heart, but it is the Lord's purpose that prevails,'" she recited.

Max kept silent.

Memories of sitting in a stiff pew during Sunday services came back in a blink. He'd tried, but he'd never pleased God as a child. He never pleased God as an adult, either. Where was the path to peace God promised? It remained elusive.

The successes Max had achieved hadn't been enough. Thus, at the age of twenty-five, he'd given up on religion.

As far as his career, he sometimes wondered if he was on the right path. Was his research nothing more than a "fluffy" elective for uninterested college freshmen? Society seemed to think along those lines, and reports through the academic grapevine whispered that ornithology programs were soon to be scrapped.

Sure, Max was appreciated—which was the reason why he was in hamster-wheel performance mode—to continue proving himself to his colleagues.

"Gerry and I are in a band," he replied, when he realized Dorothy waited for him to say something. "We rehearse online."

"Online?" Her brow furrowed.

"You're a professional, so you expect frequent in-person rehearsals. But our band rehearses virtually every week. Technology is marvelous, isn't it?"

"Not as rewarding as live rehearsals, though."

Max had to agree. "There's a likelihood Gerry and I will perform this month, if we can find a venue."

"Inquire at The Garden Terrace restaurant. The owners book entertainment on Friday evenings. In addition, I'd be delighted to host you here at the store. Do you have any CDs for sale?"

"You're kidding, right?"

"What's the name of your band?"

"The Bearded Elves."

"Hmm. Neither of you sports a beard."

"We change our name with the season."

She grinned. "When February hits, you'll become ..."

"The Bearded Valentines. But I won't be here in February. My work takes me all over the US, and I'm headed to Florida in January."

"Well, I look forward to hearing you perform this month."

"Thanks. Gerry encouraged me to rent a place in Cherish. He believes all this down-home goodness is beneficial for me."

"You're on a vacation the entire month?"

"I'm rarely on vacation."

"No wife or children?" Pointedly, she peered at his left hand.

"Neither. You're looking at a forty-year-old bachelor."

She granted a conspiratorial smile. "The right woman will come along and change your mind."

"I doubt it. Women can be ... exasperating."

She chuckled. "Will you travel to New York for Christmas?"

"I'll spend Christmas day with Gerry, his wife, Melissa, and their newborn colicky son. They're first-time parents."

Dorothy rolled her eyes. "So I've heard."

Besides Gerry, there was no one else, Max thought. Unless Max's foster brother, John, who resided in a faraway Portuguese village, counted.

It didn't matter. The season had lost its meaning eons ago. December twenty-fifth was just another day that passed in the flicker of an eye.

Dorothy's fixed smile didn't vacillate. She seemed the sort who put immense emphasis on the holidays.

He shifted. "I'm grateful for the opportunity to hunker down with my research this month."

At Dorothy's quizzical glance, he added, "On birds."

"Along with performing a live gig or two."

"Gerry and I aren't expert musicians like you and your husband, or that Slater worship singer guy. Our specialty is performing at roadside diners for a free meal."

"I well remember those days." She shook her head. "Since you'll be working here for the month, do you need any assistance with your research?"

"Can you recommend someone who could go birding with me tomorrow morning? I'd appreciate a guide."

Dorothy studied him. "I picture you in a forest, somewhere more suited to your rugged looks, rather than writing papers. You must spend a great deal of time outdoors."

"I try." He pushed a hand through his thick hair. When

had he last gotten it cut? "The Carolinas have various bird species I'd like to listen to."

"Your parakeets will truly mimic other birds?"

"Optimistically, although I haven't had much luck with them imitating anything."

Except "God bless us, every one."

"I know the ideal woman," Dorothy said.

"She likes nature?"

"Absolutely, and she's passionate about hiking." A gleam of mischief shone in Dorothy's eyes. "She works at Thumbs Up, a local florist, but might be off tomorrow. I'll text her."

"What's her name?"

"Sarah Hartman." Dorothy snatched a cell phone from beneath the counter. "She dropped out of college to care for her elderly aunt, then went on to pursue a degree in floral design."

"How old is she?"

"Sarah turned thirty last month. She's the type who juggles a half dozen projects, numerous details, and never gets frustrated. And ..." Dorothy paused to accentuate the words. "Her flower arrangements are exquisite."

He'd never purchased store-bought flowers in his life. The most magnificent blossoms—miniature red roses, deep violets, and pale blue ivy—spilled alongside brooks or grew wild in a field.

A response flew across Dorothy's phone screen. "Sarah confirmed she's not working until tomorrow afternoon," Dorothy read. "She had plans but is happy to change them. What's your address, Max?"

"I rented a house a couple blocks from here. It's 8 Poplar Lane. Tell her I'll bring the hiking essentials."

Dorothy typed into her phone, then delivered the response. "She'll pick you up in the morning."

"A hiker and a florist is an attractive combination."

"Oh, and she's plenty more. Animals love her. The cat at the greenhouse that handles mice won't let anyone near her except Sarah. Likewise, dogs practically grovel at her feet." Dorothy glanced up. "Remember Molly Belle?"

"Your brother's unruly dog?"

Dorothy choked a giggle. "She adores everyone and is beyond energetic, although remarkably calm and obedient around Sarah."

"Does Sarah own any pets?"

"Are you giving away birds?"

"I'd never part with my parakeets. Angel is the oldest, and she's been with me for several years." He lifted a quizzical brow. "What about Sarah?"

"She owns a few animals."

"Is she married?" He didn't want an irate husband or boyfriend on his tail for going birdwatching with Sarah.

"She's coming off a sorry relationship, but you'll discover she's a stunner."

Another word for mantrap. He understood the type well after dating a flirtatious woman who'd been beautiful enough to be on the cover of *Vogue* but who abruptly ended their month of dating with a cursory text.

From that point forward, he'd avoided any romantic overtures from beautiful women. They were interested in a guy's money and power. As soon as they realized Max had neither, they hightailed it out of his life.

"You'll learn all about her tomorrow." Dorothy peered at the phone screen, grinned, then snapped it shut. "She drives a yellow pickup truck and said she'll see you at eight."

CHAPTER TWO

The following day, Max rose before dawn to wash and dry the parakeets' food bowls and water bottles, then placed a slice of kiwi in their cages. Angel, a female, occupied her own cage, while the two males shared a cage.

"God bless us, every one," Angel chirped.

Max covered three sides of the wrought-iron cage and faced her on the open side. Over and over, he enunciated, "Angel. Angel. Angel."

"God bless us, every one," Angel repeated.

"You can say that entire sentence, but you can't pronounce your own name?" He threw his hands up and surveyed the other two parakeets. The blue-winged roommates perched on their respective swings, then burst into a flurry of activity for no apparent reason, effectively distracting Angel.

And thus, the lesson was over.

Max choked on a laugh. Some things never changed.

Regardless, he was in jovial spirits. Although his new bed was lumpy and the bedspread a musty chenille, he had slept well and left his window open a crack. The whisper of a floral-scented breeze had provided him with a comfortable, peaceful slumber.

He flicked a fatigued glance at his handwritten notes, twenty pages and counting, spread out on the computer desk. His suitcases still sat on the floor, waiting to be unpacked. He'd rummaged through them for a clean pair of jeans, a blue button-down shirt, boots, and his favorite bow tie.

A half hour after he'd showered and passed on shaving because he couldn't find his razor, he heard an engine and peered out the window.

A yellow pickup idled in the driveway. The truck boasted reindeer antlers attached to the windows and a red nose on the front grill.

The woman in the driver's seat caught his stare and waved, her smile bright and pleasant.

Sarah Hartman, he assumed. Punctual at eight o'clock in the morning.

Admirable. They were off to a promising start.

He filled a thermos with fresh coffee and stuffed thermal cups, peanut-butter banana sandwiches, and his favorite brand of frosted sugar cookies in a bag. Hoisting a backpack over his shoulders, he headed outside.

He opened the passenger door, smiling in at her. "Sarah, right?" he said. He put the food bag and his backpack in the back seat, then slid onto the passenger seat.

"Correct." She nodded to him. "And you're Max?"

"Indeed. Max Archer." He set his thermos in the truck's oversized cup holder. "And you're driving Rudolph."

She laughed, gentle and musical. "I love Christmas."

"Let me guess, you're a sentimental movie junkie too." He gestured to her glittery pine tree earrings and the white snowflake steering wheel cover.

"Sentimental movies are the best." She tilted her head,

studying him with sea-green eyes. "You look exactly the way Dorothy described."

"Not a reindeer covered in snowflakes, I hope?"

She swallowed a chuckle. "No."

"How did Dorothy describe me?"

Sarah stared at his lips. "She said you had dark hair, silvery-gray eyes, wore a bow tie and would probably have a backpack."

"A battered and weathered one." He twisted and motioned to his backpack, its ripped seam fixed with duct tape. "Today, it's filled with necessities—bottles of water, a first-aid kit, binoculars, and my fully charged phone."

She nodded. "Sounds like you've got everything you need."

"Yes. I've brought my microphone and recorder too. To record birdsongs, I'll demonstrate the setup when we arrive at the mountain."

"Okay."

"Are you carrying a cellphone?" he asked.

"I always carry one for emergencies, but I also use my phone camera to take photos."

"Photos of wildlife?"

"Mostly deer, although I can never get closer than fifteen feet before they bolt."

"Deer aren't always the sweet, docile animals you may imagine. Be careful around them."

"I am."

Those green eyes fringed with thick russet lashes, and her creamy complexion, enhanced by light freckles across her nose, stopped him from responding with anything other than "Good."

She continued to watch him, and he returned her stare.

This beautiful, intelligent woman hadn't been scooped up by a guy?

Wearing a hooded red jacket, gloves, and brown hiking

boots, she was small and slim. He estimated no taller than five feet. He found himself staring at her delicate lips before his gaze wandered down to the silver cross necklace around her slender neck.

Preoccupied with an attraction he hadn't expected, he picked up his thermos. "Another requirement for a morning outing is caffeine. Do you like black coffee?"

She nodded.

"Then we share commonalities—coffee and hiking. I also brought a package of cookies. They're store-bought because I'm not a baker. The cookies, not the coffee." He returned his thermos to the holder. "Juniper Mountain is our first stop."

"There's another?"

"Crandall's Mountain, depending on our time frame."

"Okay. My morning is free," she replied.

"Mine too."

With a quick bob of her head, she backed out of the driveway.

He stretched out his legs. "It will be good to go for a long hike. I arrived in town yesterday, driving down from New York. I'm here for the month, then heading for a job in Florida."

Another nod. She probably already knew that because of chatty Dorothy.

Because he liked to have music playing, he asked her if he could switch on the radio. She hesitated and then said yes, and he scanned the stations, on a quest for something other than a holiday tune. He settled on Jon Bon Jovi singing "Please Come Home For Christmas." Not typically merry, but more of an expressive classic.

Satisfied, Max drew out his cellphone. "Do you need directions to the mountain?"

She twisted. "Say that again?"

"Directions?" He spoke louder.

"No. I've hiked Juniper for years. It's part of the Carolina state park systems."

"I mapped the distance to Crandall's, because the mountains are within a few miles of each other."

Another glance. He repeated that Juniper and Crandall were near each other.

Each time he talked, she swiveled to look at him. At one point, he almost advised her to watch the road, not him.

He lowered the volume on the radio. Possibly, music distracted her when she drove.

"I brought a knapsack," she said after a few silent minutes. "It's on the back seat."

Don't turn around to show me, Max silently implored.

He didn't initiate any further dialogue, spending the time glancing sideways at her appealing profile.

After they arrived at Juniper Mountain and she parked, they got out of the truck and he poured two cups of coffee, handing her one. He grabbed a swallow, pleased the coffee was still hot, and scanned their surroundings.

Today might provide a breakthrough in his research, an ultimate realization of success. That is, if his parakeets cooperated and actually repeated the birdsongs.

He gazed at the gorgeous woman beside him, leaning against her truck, and smiled. Surely, Sarah would bring good fortune.

When they finished their coffees, they detoured to the visitor center and procured a map. Sarah lingered at a Christmas ornament display, sputtering in disbelief when the park ranger stated that the store was sold out of a particular ornament featuring a bear, hiker boots and the inscription, "Take a hike."

She pointed to an exhibit on the wall. "The ornament is hanging right there and will go perfect on my holiday tree."

"Those are display items only and can't be sold," the

ranger responded. "More should arrive by the end of the month. Check back."

She stuffed her gloves in her pockets and tapped her fingers on the counter. "By then, Christmas will be over."

Eager to lighten the mood, Max steered her out the exit to a wooden bench. "Let's study the map. There are eleven trails." He beckoned her to sit and settled beside her, indicating a twisty pathway. "The Maple Tree route is strenuous with rocky terrain and unsuitable for beginners."

"Fortunately, I'm not a beginner," she replied matter-of-factly.

"Neither am I."

"Maple Tree isn't difficult, but I recommend ..." She ran her finger along a trail marked Oak. "This one passes through Walnut Forest, down to the Nanchee River's edge, up through a meadow, and finishes on a grassy path leading back to the visitor center."

She peered at him for a deciding opinion.

Based on the fact she'd resided in Cherish for many years, Max readily approved.

With her so close, her scent reminded him of an elusive flowery fragrance, similar to the breeze floating through his window last night. Rosewood, perhaps. Peaceful and serene.

He liked that. He liked *her*.

Their gazes merged, and he couldn't stop staring. She was stunning—high cheekbones and a flawless complexion—the type of beauty that prompted people to gape.

"You're the expert in these parts, Sarah." Max thought he spoke, but he wasn't certain, because the world had become unfocused, and she was at the center. He moved his index finger alongside hers, along the map, a light brush of fingertips.

And the attraction. His heart did a backflip.

He forced himself to concentrate on the map and swallowed. Surely, she felt it too.

An easy smile worked its way across her features.

Was she interested in him?

With any luck, she was.

At the same instant his brain shouted no, no, no. He was here for research purposes, and Sarah Hartman was a romantic complication he could ill afford. He had enough conflicts in his life—a stressful job, and no relationship at all with religion. Her necklace signified she was a Christian, and before he knew it, she might be declaring, "'This is the day that the Lord has made.'"

He'd believed that psalm once upon a time. Not anymore.

He pulled his extra pair of binoculars from his backpack and handed them to her, then hung his own around his neck. Next, he retrieved his recording device, a pocket-sized digital recorder and the microphone.

She rose. He automatically stood too.

"Your gear is more sophisticated than I envisioned."

"After years of trial and error, I finally realized my equipment had to be top of the line." He plugged the module into a mini jack cable. "The shotgun microphone has a powering module containing a battery."

She gazed at him with wide eyes and a wider smile. "I'm impressed with you and your work, Max."

"I'm impressed by you too," he replied.

"I haven't done anything remarkable."

He pressed his fingers on her forearm, lightly, to make his point. "There aren't many women who'd change their plans to assist a newcomer in town."

"I'm always happy to help."

He told himself to finish readying the equipment rather than gaze at her lovely, upturned face. He covered the microphone with a wind sock. "This reduces the noise created by the wind."

She acknowledged his description with a nod.

He scanned the sky, checking the angle of the sun. The haze was beginning to clear, gray clouds giving way to shades of pink and lavender. "Sunny days are ideal, but overcast is also fine," he said.

In the wash of the morning light, her complexion glowed. "Birding is a first for me."

"I was under the impression you're an animal lover."

"I am. Usually, I bring my dogs here."

"How many?"

"I have two dogs."

He noted her smile. "Is something amusing, Sarah?"

"I was thinking you're remarkably efficient and obviously an expert in your profession. I admire a man who makes things look easy and effortless."

Her compliment caught him off balance. He uttered a heartfelt, "Birds are my life and my career."

A December breeze rustled the trees and blew her shiny hair across her face. He smoothed an auburn lock from her cheek, and she stepped back out of his range.

"In any case ..." He cleared his throat and passed her a protein bar.

"Is this lunch?"

"I packed sandwiches. This is a snack."

Before he could say anything else, she whispered a prayer, asking God to bless their food, Max's career, and the picturesque day.

Max scratched his neck. Nothing made him feel more like a fraud than thanking an imagined God. For what? A protein bar? A clear day?

God had never granted any of Max's requests.

Nevertheless, he bent his head and studied the protein bar's wrapper while Sarah prayed.

After finishing with an amen, she said, "I love animals too," as if their conversation hadn't been stalled by prayer.

His response was a dull nod.

She nodded to the knapsack on her shoulders. "Are you interested in what's inside?"

He took a bite of the protein bar. "Sure."

"I have sunscreen and used tea bags."

At his questioning look, she clarified, "Tea bags are a natural alternative to commercial products and will ease the sting of bug bites. Or, for instance, if you walk into a poison ivy plant."

"A person doesn't walk into a poison ivy plant."

"Sure they do. At least, I have."

He grinned. "We're both protected and covered." He surveyed her hooded jacket and jeans. For a petite woman, her legs were long and shapely.

"A slight brush of poison ivy leaves on your skin is all it takes for a rash," she said.

"I'll protect you."

She wrinkled her nose. "From poison ivy?"

"From anything." Protectiveness for her stirred inside him, an unforeseen response. He'd blurted the words aloud before forming the thought in his mind.

Her dubious gaze leveled on him.

"You don't believe me?" he asked.

"We hardly know each other, and I certainly don't need protecting. In addition, I packed bear repellent."

"I doubt we'll come across any bears."

"Let's hope not, but just in case." She withdrew a soup can from her knapsack and shook it. "It's full of pebbles and makes a handy noisemaker."

"A bear weighs a lot more than we do, and we can't outrun one. Bear that in mind." He chuckled. "Pun intended."

The joke seemed to slide past her. "I've read about bear encounters," she answered. "There are certain rules to remember, such as to speak calmly, not make direct eye contact, and never run."

"If your handy deterrent doesn't scare away a bear, the loud noise will no doubt encourage any birds in the area to take flight."

"That's not a good thing if you're trying to record bird-songs," she replied with a grin.

They burst out laughing, then started down a gravel trail.

He stood on the forest's edge and watched for motion. "Look. Listen. There's a golden-winged warbler in the trees." He raised his binoculars and encouraged Sarah to do the same.

She regarded him blankly.

He held up his microphone and began recording. "The warbler has suffered the steepest decline of any songbird."

"Why?"

"Loss of habitat for breeding."

A sharp *chip* and a melodic *warble* diverted him. He signaled toward a metal-gray and yellow bird hopping between bushes in a cluster of thick ferns.

"You're hearing an adult male Canada warbler," he said.

"Oh."

Oh? *Oh?*

"Some people pish to encourage birdsong." He imitated the sound. "I don't. I've found birds will come out no matter what and I wait for their natural behavior."

As they continued along the path, he was absorbed in recording and figuring out what birds he heard, and Sarah offered no help in identifying any of them. Every few minutes, the hushed air was fragmented by a high-pitched cry, and Max stopped to record.

Well into their walk, an outbreak of wings sounded louder than the crunch of leaves beneath their feet. Before he raised his binoculars, a bird flew out of range and into the brush. Max skimmed the shorter branches to find the bird, disregarding a group of energetic high school students breezing by with their teacher guide.

A second stir of motion in his peripheral vision had Max rushing to record.

Each clue necessitated an intermission, an awaiting, a heeding.

The appeal of ornithology. Search and find.

Max had become engrossed in the study of birds when Mr. Lenny, a foster parent, had brought him birding. He was a kind man with wavy gray hair and tortoise-rimmed eyeglasses. He was the only adult who'd shown a true interest in Max, and they started a tradition of birding every Saturday morning. For a child with precious few traditions, the man was a father figure. Lenny had made a lasting impression, inspiring a young boy who had no real home.

A woodpecker ripping through the brush, accompanied by three cardinals singing *cheer*, *cheer*, *cheer*, snapped Max out of his reminiscing. He spun and monitored their calls, tiptoeing through the undergrowth, peering above and below.

Sarah, on the other hand, seemed anxious to move on. She pointed her binoculars skyward and rarely spoke.

That is until they reached the Nanchee River's edge.

"An ideal spot for a picnic." Max nodded to the waterfall beyond and fished in his bag for sandwiches.

The weather had changed, and clouds covered the sky.

"I'll keep my cellphone handy," Sarah remarked, "in case I see a deer."

A crash came from somewhere he couldn't pinpoint. Max

whirled around, searching for the source, and glimpsed a large animal emerging from the river.

"I can finally take a close-up photo of a deer," Sarah declared. She stepped toward the river, but slipped on a patch of wet grass and clung to his hand.

It wasn't a deer, Max thought. A deer would shy away.

It was a bear. A wandering yearling male by Max's estimate.

The bear started for them on all fours.

Sarah's breath burst—an inhale, an exhale.

Seconds froze.

"Where's your deterrent?" Max abandoned his equipment and drew her close. She grabbed her knapsack and pulled out the soup can.

The bear came up on hind legs, almost eye to eye with them, and with one hand, Max flung his peanut butter sandwiches, the cookies, and the protein bars as far as he could. Sarah shook the can, yelled, and tossed it near the bear.

The bear backed away, then turned and ran.

Sarah licked her trembling lips, her eyes damp. "Thank you, God."

Max kept his arm around her tight shoulders and provided a reassuring squeeze. His heartbeat raced, his mouth dry. "We're safe."

"These things happen in books and movies. Not to real people." She attempted a feeble stab at humor.

Despite her ashen complexion, he was impressed she'd lost none of her composure and had reacted quickly. Still, her rounded green eyes shone luminous beneath her russet, delicate eyebrows.

Max didn't have a boatload of experience with women, but he'd lived with enough foster sisters to know when a female was on the brink of tears. Sarah bravely tried to hold them at bay, blinking ferociously.

He wavered between his male instinct to sidestep any prospect of a sobbing woman—or the reasonable desire to offer support.

Her lips parted, her smile sluggish. "Countless questions are running through my mind," she said quietly.

"Let's begin with the most important. Are you okay?"

"Yes." He heard the quiver in her tone. "We've established we're both fine."

He lifted her chin. "Let's celebrate how grateful we are."

"By prayer?"

"A consideration for a Christian, I assume, but I thought of something more like this." He brought her closer. Unhurried, he kissed her.

Her expressive eyes gazed into his. When she veered, his hands tightened, and his mouth moved more firmly.

"Max."

"Hmm?" he murmured.

The air was hushed, the only sound the babbling river.

She slid her fingers up the collar of his jacket. "Nothing." Hesitant, she returned his kiss.

Max got so caught up in kissing Sarah, a moment went by before boisterous talking penetrated his brain. He lifted his head and glimpsed the same high schoolers from earlier.

With a self-conscious shift, Sarah pulled from his grasp. "I see we have company," she said.

"Right." *And at a most inopportune moment.*

He darted a glance at his watch, retrieved his equipment, and pushed out a sigh. "I suppose we should head back."

As they retraced their steps, Sarah glanced up at him. "Max, I can't believe ..."

"I wanted to kiss you as soon as I saw you this morning," he said.

She bit her lip. "Did we do everything right?"

"The kiss was perfect."

A rosy blush tinted her cheeks. "I'm referring to the bear."

He chuckled. "All I remember is throwing food at him."

"Thank you for protecting me."

He hadn't, really. If anything, *she* had protected *him*, protected them *both*, with her bear deterrent.

"Thank *you*." He reached for her hand, soft and delicate, and a rush of emotion made him smile.

In silence, they returned to her truck.

Still dazed by the whirl of emotions between their fear and the resulting kiss, they spoke little on the drive back to Cherish. Max didn't bring up hiking Crandall's Mountain, and he kept the radio off.

When she pulled into the driveway of his home, he didn't encourage her to join him birding again. Nor did he invite her inside—something he had considered along the entire route.

"The sandwiches are gone," he said. "Sorry. No lunch."

"We could have been lunch for the bear."

"Thankfully, we weren't. Besides, he was young and not very aggressive."

"Even when he charged straight for us?"

"He's undoubtedly partying right now, devouring cookies and sandwiches and protein bars with his friends." Max tried a laugh, then sobered. "Sorry you didn't get a picture of a deer."

"I took a rapid sequence of photos with my cellphone."

"Did they come out?"

"I haven't had the opportunity to check yet."

"You had time. I knew we were safe all along," Max declared.

"Uh, huh." She became absorbed in tracing the pattern of snowflakes on her steering wheel. "As long as the bear didn't swat the ground with his front paw."

"Or snort," Max countered.

"Or lunge."

He answered with a smile. She was lovely, amiable, and attractive, and his instinctive reaction was to lean over and kiss her again.

However, other instincts warned to keep his distance. A short-term romance didn't benefit anyone, and Sarah deserved more. With his relentless studies, travel, and limited financial resources, he had little to offer her.

He told himself he was wed to his profession, as a girl-friend from long ago had once accused him.

The mood in the truck became quieter.

Let's face it, he reasoned. Sarah wasn't excited about his profession, anyway. She'd responded to his interest with little more than a few nods. Birding was his passion, and he wanted someone to share his enthusiasm.

Satisfied with his decision, he grabbed his backpack and opened the passenger door. "Thanks for the ride and for being my guide. Have a marvelous afternoon."

Their experience would be remembered as a memorable exploration. A couple hikers who scored a birding, or rather, a bear adventure.

And their kiss? Yes, there was that. Delightful, tender, and exquisite.

Like Sarah.

CHAPTER THREE

*A*fter dropping Max off, Sarah stopped by her home to tend to her animals before continuing on to Thumbs Up, the nursery/garden center where she worked.

To her intense relief, the garden center's parking lot was nearly empty. Many customers, particularly older gardeners, preferred to shop for plants in the morning. She blew out a thankful breath. She needed the quiet to revisit her moments with Max.

She'd admired his home when she drove up to the neat and tidy rental, encouraged that he didn't have a bird perched on his shoulder as she'd half imagined.

Dorothy had texted Sarah the previous evening, detailing Max's plans. He didn't intend to stay in Cherish forever—only a month to explore the area for information supporting his research.

December is an unusual month for research, Sarah had texted, *considering the holidays.*

Apparently, any close family is nonexistent, Dorothy replied. *Plus, I asked if he was married and he isn't.*

Sarah could scarcely believe that the brilliant, handsome

man, his muscular physique filling out his twill jacket, was so approachable.

On closer range, his eyes, brimming with kindness, shone light silver beneath dark, straight eyebrows. His hair was thick and longish, and she was tempted to brush back the waves that constantly fell across his forehead.

Of course, she didn't. They hardly knew each other.

Besides his intellect (she'd looked up his profile on an ornithology university website), he was amicable, humorous and thoughtful. She made the blunder of staring at him often to hear his words more clearly, and her gaze had been drawn to his firm mouth.

Then the kiss had happened.

Oh my, such a kiss! At first, she'd been tentative and self-conscious at their closeness. His mouth had sought hers with cool expertise, then persistence, then increasing claim. Her heart had responded in rapid, thudding beats.

If the teenagers hadn't entered the scene, would she still be kissing him?

Her cheeks warmed. They must have seen her and Max together.

Almost unwillingly, Max had lifted his head to end the kiss.

A kiss she never should have allowed. What an impru-dent, impulsive thing for her to do—in the middle of a public state park.

Yet, his lips had been persuasive and tender.

A part of her insisted she should have ended the kiss first. The other part maintained that she and Max had shared a distressing incident. Subsequently, their mutual fright had drawn them closer.

When the bear came upon them, Max had held her. He'd kept his promise, prepared to protect her.

Once they had begun the hike, Max had been fixated on

his work. For her, the birdcalls that excited him had been faint and distant.

Why?

Why couldn't she hear the birds Max was obviously eager to record? He was so in tune with them.

Lately, she'd found that if she didn't watch people's lips while they spoke, she sometimes missed what they said.

Regardless, she appreciated Max's spontaneity, fairly bouncing on his toes as he dashed through the brush. She was accustomed to sitting on the sidelines. Her loud, raucous, older brothers had consistently stolen the spotlight, and her parents often overlooked her.

She fingered the silver cross on her neck.

Max gave the impression of being uncomfortable when she offered a prayer before eating, whereas she was a Christian and faith was important to her. By his quick exit when she'd taken him home, he obviously wasn't interested in her, anyway.

As she always did in moments of confusion, she turned to God to set her course.

The psalmist in Proverbs 4:23 had written, "Above all else, guard your heart, for everything you do flows from it."

She'd had her heart broken by a budding architect. Their relationship had ended quickly, although she'd wept for days. Since then, her emotions were precarious at best.

Nonetheless, she'd vowed to reset her path after that painful experience. Her heart wouldn't be broken a second time. Not even by Max.

Her eyes squeezed shut, and she uttered a prayer. "God, set me free from my reservations and uncertainty. Please show me the way." She always felt better after praying. Her God was a big God, bigger than her hurts and disappointments.

Taking an easy breath, she exited her truck and pushed opened the nursery's heavy steel doors.

"Good afternoon, Sarah." Bonnie Ellerman, a coworker, tapped Sarah on the shoulder. "You're fifteen minutes early. I'm on register today, and you're working the floor. The amaryllis flowers are thriving, and timing the bulbs to bloom for Christmas worked like a charm. No wonder the garden center relies on your expertise. You have a magical green thumb."

"Hardly magical." Sarah tied a blue employee apron around her waist. "If the rest period for the amaryllis begins in late summer, the bulbs will respond. Customers appreciate the extensive blooms, thus it's worth all the planning."

Sarah picked up a warehouse broom to sweep soil off the concrete floor. She tackled the chores she disliked first, before arranging the pink, white, and red poinsettia plants for Memorial Street Church.

An unexpected thickness formed in her throat as she gazed at the tastefully decorated Christmas trees lining an entire side wall. The prospect of returning home to spend another night by herself during the Christmas season ... during any season ... Well, she yearned for more.

To cheer herself up, she organized a Christmas gift list in her mind. Uncle Gerry, her great-uncle in Perrytown, played guitar. Accordingly, a gift from Musically Yours would be ideal.

An insistent voice in Sarah's ear interrupted her thoughts as Dorothy Edwards came into view.

"Hello," Dorothy said. "I stopped by to purchase a pink poinsettia plant for Musically Yours." Dorothy grinned mischievously, and Sarah knew at once that Dorothy had come into the nursery for more than a poinsettia.

"Who's minding your music store?" Sarah asked with a chuckle.

"Emmanuelle." Dorothy changed the poinsettia from one arm to the other. "So, how was your hike together?"

Sarah quirked an eyebrow. "With ..."

"Maxwell Archer."

"Enjoyable."

"That's it?"

"That's it." A wry smile touched Sarah's lips as she navigated the subject back to Dorothy. "Is Ryan in Atlanta?"

"He's preparing for a classical concert there. He's the lead in a chamber choir and singing a sacred text in Latin. The concert will be live-streamed next weekend." Dorothy paused. "You know I love gushing about my husband's accomplishments, but now I want to find out about your date details."

"Hiking a mountain is hardly a date." Sarah attempted to compose her features and disguise her attraction to Max. He was so different from the architect she'd dated, who'd had arrogant qualities and a slight build. Max, on the other hand, exuded strong masculinity. He was also smart, passionate about his work and gentlemanly.

And the kiss.

The sigh-worthy kiss.

Animated chatter from customers swirled nearer, blending with the clink of a clay pot as Bonnie handed Sarah a paperwhite narcissus and requested a price check.

Dorothy trailed Sarah to the stand of blossoming paperwhites. "What are your thoughts regarding Max?"

Sarah focused on Dorothy's mouth in order to lip-read.

She'd been ignoring the polite remarks from friends about having her hearing checked. A woman of thirty was *not* hard of hearing. For the time being, she'd employ all the tools at her disposal, and one was lipreading.

"He seems nice," she replied.

"Nice. Nice?' Dorothy flung a hand to her hip. "What sort of description is *nice* for a handsome, well-versed man?"

"He's well-versed on birds." Sarah gave Dorothy a good-natured shove. "Period."

Well, no, that should probably be a comma. He was also well-versed on kindness. Similarly, he's sweet and understanding, with a romantic nature she hadn't anticipated.

"I can tell by your reddened cheeks there's more to the story." Dorothy smothered a laugh. "You're attracted to him."

"He's polite and humorous." Sarah's gaze veered to Bonnie, who was frantically signaling another employee over to the narcissus plants.

Sarah's attention swung back to Dorothy.

"Am I right?" Dorothy asked, grinning.

"Maybe."

"I knew it!" Dorothy's expression went from happy to happier.

"My reactions are mixed. He's brilliant, yes—"

"Plus, he's an animal lover, just like you."

"Let's not forget he's taking a position at a Florida university in January."

"Yes, yes." Dorothy moved to the side to allow the employee to pass. "You actually start working here at one, right?"

Sarah nodded.

"So, we have a couple more minutes. Have you considered adopting the adorable dog that Nicholas and the Cherish sheriff department are caring for? An officer is complaining they are on call 24/7. The dog has a tremendous appetite and eats a lot of puppy chow."

"Have they named him yet?"

"They're waiting for the right person to adopt him. We all agree you are the perfect new owner."

"Who are we?"

"Me, Nicholas, and Emmanuelle."

"I adopted two abandoned dogs, two cats, a goldfish and a hamster," Sarah said. "Plus, my house is a one-story bungalow."

"You'll adore him when you see him."

"I'm touched, and would love to help ... but I can't."

Dorothy sighed. "Notify Nicholas if you change your mind. Deal?"

"Deal."

"One more thing." Dorothy glanced at her watch at the same time Sarah did.

"Go on."

Dorothy pulled in a breath. "One of the reasons Max decided to stay in Cherish this month is because he's friends with Gerry."

Sarah stumbled back a step. "My great-uncle Gerry?"

"The men play in a band together. Max told me when he was in my store yesterday to buy a harmonica."

"Uncle Gerry never discussed Max before. How long have they been friends?"

Dorothy winked. "Ask Max."

With that, Dorothy waltzed to the cash register with her blooming pink poinsettia.

Sarah was left staring at the paperwhite in her hand, trying to remember Bonnie's request. Was the flower supposed to be restocked or bedecked with a ribbon?

No, no. A price check. But another worker had taken care of it.

Sarah stifled a quiet moan. Her focus was fractured. And all because of a man named Maxwell Archer. A sensitive, fascinating and accomplished man.

And then another thought formed.

Perhaps, just perhaps, she could enlist her great-uncle's help to meet Max again.

With a radiant smile and a lively step, Sarah clocked into work at exactly one o'clock.

CHAPTER FOUR

A week later, Max strode into his living room and ducked as Angel flew by. He allowed the parakeets to fly at least an hour a day and kept the doors and windows closed for their safety. The routine kept them healthy and happy because they needed to explore. He'd limited their time the first week, in order for them to get used to the unfamiliar environment of the rental.

For now, the roommates were back in their cages, which left only Angel perching on a curtain rod. He'd trained the budgies to return to their cages, but Angel sometimes preferred not to.

Earlier, Max had compiled his notes and organized the pages in a computer file. He'd worked eighteen-hour days all week, although emailing his file to the ornithology department in Florida hadn't produced the desired accolades. The university had demanded additional bird recordings—particularly of his budgies repeating the birdsongs.

Except his birds hadn't responded or repeated any of the songs.

After Max received the university's reply, he didn't trust

himself to respond. His ideal job. How could the department question him?

Perhaps he was in the wrong profession after all. Published studies demanded reliable facts, and budgies, as well as birds in general, were unpredictable.

Budgies mimicked humans and the sounds of their mates. However, their response to his recordings had brought distress and frustration. They peered around, attempting to establish where the birdsongs came from. When they failed to locate their perceived new friends whom they suspected were close by, they became anxious.

Max contemplated his options.

He wouldn't return to New York City, and the Florida university position didn't seem as appealing anymore, considering the head of the ornithology group wanted Max to work round the clock for little pay.

At any rate, another hike to Juniper Mountain was in Max's forecast. He considered contacting Sarah and asking her to accompany him.

During the past seven days, he'd given the morning they'd spent together deeper consideration. He remembered her face going pale when the bear charged. He also recalled how sweet she was, and how fearless. He admired her beauty, but was more intrigued by her modest and steady presence. She'd bravely held back frightened tears after scaring off the bear.

Society sometimes displayed a cynical indifference to the wonders of nature, but Sarah appreciated the unspoiled forest. He had recognized the romantic interest whenever she gazed at him, and it melted him with surprising tenderness as he recalled their affectionate kiss.

And how did he repay her kindness after she'd given up her morning to hike with him?

Why, he'd departed with a quick, "Thanks for the ride and for being my guide. Have a marvelous afternoon."

Who said such words after sharing a morning with a beautiful woman?

Apparently, he did.

He rubbed a hand over his face. After their tender kiss, what must she think of him? Their hours shouldn't have ended with such finality. He blamed his cool farewell on the fact that he was weary after the lengthy drive, his move, and endless unpacking.

Nevertheless, he needed to rectify any misunderstanding because she fascinated him.

But how?

He lifted a cup of wassail to his lips and swallowed, and a familiar comfort surged through him. Years earlier, Mr. Lenny's wife, Amanda, had mixed homemade wassail using ingredients on hand—apple, orange, and cranberry juice.

Ultimately, Max had come to realize those long-ago times of assembling in Lenny's cheery kitchen drinking wassail with him, his wife, and their son, John, had resulted in Max's fantasy of heart-warming holidays surrounded by loved ones.

That fantasy never materialized. Still, he felt a sense of allegiance and gratitude to Lenny that exceeded every other emotion. Which was why, he supposed, he drank wassail.

A few short months after Max's placement with Lenny and his family, Max had been returned to his birth mother's care until she was hospitalized with liver disease. By then, the water and electricity in their apartment had been shut off. He never learned what happened to his father, who had never been a part of Max's life.

A loud knock on the front door sounded, and Gerry's voice bellowed, "Anyone home?"

"Just me and a bird flying around the living room."

A snicker. "You've been around birds so long you learned to fly?"

"Hang on while I catch Angel."

"Will it take a while?"

"Anywhere from five minutes to an hour, depending on if she cooperates."

A loud guffaw. "The weather is comfortable and I'll wait on the porch. I brought you a housewarming gift. A bottle of blackberry brandy."

"Really? I don't normally drink brandy ... but thanks."

From experience, Max knew coaxing Angel to her cage was no easy task. Parakeets were flock animals, and keenly aware of a person's body language. They were, after all, low man on the food chain and had learned to be cautious.

Max chatted quietly and walked nonchalantly, coaxing her down from the curtain rod. After he picked her up, he held his hand lightly over her wings and carried her to her cage.

A half hour later, he and Gerry sat in Max's tiny kitchen drinking cups of wassail. Gerry poured a shot of blackberry brandy into his cup, claiming he needed something to calm his nerves, being a spanking new father and all.

Max declined the brandy. He wanted to keep his wits about him while he engaged with the birds. Tonight, he planned on playing the harmonica—perhaps a scale followed by a soulful ballade. Maybe they would mimic the musical sounds.

He leaned back in his stool as Gerry brought him up to date on living with a newborn and how he embraced fatherhood in his fifties. Then Gerry poured himself another shot.

Max's initial thought upon seeing his friend in person for the first time in years was that Gerry's hair had turned a bushy stark-white—whiter than it appeared on screen—framing a robust, pink-cheeked face. His glacial-blue eyes were piercing, yet friendly. His once crusty exterior had softened.

By day, Gerry worked in a pet store in Perrytown. By night, his passion was music. Over the course of their

Internet jam sessions, Max discovered that Gerry had a powerful bass voice, and his guitar skills were disciplined and focused.

Gerry raised his cup for a toast. "To the Bearded Elves. Forever may we sing."

"Forever may we sing ... anywhere?" Max clinked cups.

"An opportunity will present itself."

"Dorothy Edwards suggested The Garden Terrace."

"We'll check it out." Gerry ran his tongue over his lips. "Hey, this is tasty wassail for a bachelor."

"Wassail is my holiday indulgence. I learned how to make it from my foster mother and father."

Max tapped a relaxed fist against his heart. "They were the epitome of kindness."

"I've known you many years, my bird singing comrade. You don't celebrate Christmas. Wassail is Christmas."

Amused, Max drank a final gulp. He too appreciated the irony of savoring wassail, rather than, say, a cold beer. Avoiding answering Gerry, he looked into the living room. The parakeets were busy quibbling with their toys and preening.

Gerry took the hint. "Any luck with the birds repeating your recorded songs?" he asked.

"None, even though I play different tracks for them every day."

"Maybe your birds would respond well if there was another animal around. I hear there is an adorable puppy in need of a home."

"A puppy galloping through my legs every morning, and keeping me up half the night?" Max shook his head. "This house is a rental, and a puppy is known to chew everything in sight. I already bumped up the place when I lugged my suit-cases inside."

"My wife and I have discussed pet ownership, but newbie

parenting is enough for now." Gerry commiserated with a nod, then gestured to the parakeets. "What do they mimic?"

Max shrugged. "Nothing."

As if on cue, Angel blurted loud and clear, "God bless us, every one."

Gerry swiveled on his stool. "Is that your bird?"

"You're hearing Angel's favorite, and only, sentence."

"Ho, ho, ho. You own a budgie who celebrates the holidays." Gerry chuckled. "Have you seen the Cherish town square transformation?"

"Too busy."

"Those little wooden houses lined up around the ten-foot Christmas tree resemble a Norman Rockwell village when lit at night. There's also a craft fair selling local wares. My wife prefers cranberry-scented candles and pine-smelling soaps."

"It's going to be challenging to shop with a newborn."

Gerry linked his hands behind his head. "Barring the matter that neither of us has slept more than three hours since little Freddie's birth, my answer is yes, it will be. Are you up for any babysitting?"

"Perhaps when he's a little older. He cries a lot?"

"He's colicky." Gerry stared into his cup, then at Max. "I thought you always wanted children."

"Someday. In the meantime, call me when he turns five."

As Gerry rambled about the egalitarian share of chores in his marriage, Max's thoughts gravitated to his research. Should he expand his study to include cardinals? A recent article by a colleague had supported a claim to include natural-history habitats, and cardinals were the state bird in neighboring North Carolina. Perhaps the Jacksonville university would be more attentive if Max's study included additional birds.

He massaged his nape. Shouldn't the ache be gone? He'd moved in a while ago.

Stress, a little voice nudged.

No. An adamant no. Stress is a motivator.

In the meantime, didn't the department head realize Max couldn't *force* his budges to talk?

"Seen the live reindeer at the children's petting zoo?" Gerry asked.

Max's musings gravitated to Sarah. She loved taking photos of deer.

Aware his friend regarded him, Max shook his head. "No time." With a weary sigh, Max picked up their cups and rinsed them in the sink. Then he led Gerry into the living room. "I'll let the birds fly around if that's okay."

"Suits me. I let my cat roam throughout my house."

"Just don't bring your cat to my house when the birds are out."

"You'll meet my new baby before you ever see my cat. I can bring little Freddie over anytime."

"Looking forward to it," Max murmured.

At the far end of the room, beyond a scarred wooden coffee table, stood a cushioned sofa and a side chair. Two large cages were hung at chest level on the opposite wall, situated near the window so the birds could see outside.

Gerry pushed his hands into his jean pockets. "I identified the recordings you sent—a golden-winged warbler and a Canada warbler."

"You're correct. You were always a top-notch student."

Gerry knew his birds. He could have found the information using birding apps, but a conscientious and deliberate Gerry most likely had done his research.

"All the birds were recorded at Juniper Mountain?" he asked.

"Yes. And the setting is superb." With an airy wave of his hand, Max gestured toward the threadbare sofa for his buddy to get comfortable, then opened the doors to the bird cages. "I enlisted the help of a local guide."

"Who?" Gerry took a seat, shooing away a bird that quickly decided to roost there. "A park ranger?"

"A woman named Sarah Hartman. She lives in Cherish and—"

"Sarah Hartman? Sarah is my great-niece."

Max stared in surprise. "You never mentioned that."

"Why would I? Our conversations center on birds and music. So, what's the consensus?" He sounded so matter-of-fact that Max grinned.

"About Sarah?"

"Who else?"

"She's lovely. Absolutely lovely." *Okay, yes, that was an understatement.* His vision of her lustrous hair cascading over her shoulders, the red highlights glistening in the sun, served as a reminder of her beauty. "And plucky. We had a close encounter with a bear and she was magnificent."

"A real live bear?"

"Big and breathing, but Sarah's quick thinking came to our rescue. She's marvelous under pressure."

"Sounds like her. She's a wunderkind with animals."

"I've heard."

Gerry leaned in. "Can I tell you something about her I've noticed lately?"

"Should you betray her confidence?"

"It's more of a speculation shared by me and a number of her friends. We believe she has a hearing deficiency she's denying."

Thoughtfully, Max nodded. That would explain her occasional hesitancy to speak and the way she kept looking at him when she was driving, as if she had trouble hearing him.

He felt a clutching in his heart. He, more than anyone, should understand. Not exactly the same, but Mr. Lenny had

worn a hearing aid, saying it helped him listen and communi-
cate—mainly in noisy situations.

Max waited while Gerry went into the kitchen and refilled
a fresh cup—all brandy and no wassail.

When he returned, he stopped short and regarded Max
for a suspiciously long time. "Well?" he prodded.

"Well, what?"

Gerry took a quick swallow of brandy. "Did you and my
divine niece get along?"

Max cleared his throat. "Of course." He turned, a clear
sign he wasn't willing to make any small talk when it came to
his feelings toward Sarah. Some subjects were personal, and
she was special.

"Alrighty then." Gerry's laughter rippled through the
room. "Next topic. Church."

"Let's close that topic before you begin." Max flipped
open his computer, scanning the files, calculating how
successfully he could change the church subject without
Gerry asking a thousand questions.

"Let me reword. Not church, necessarily, but the Cherish
church *choir*." Gerry hesitated for emphasis, his tone growing
insistent as he touched on the real issue. "A strong baritone
voice is needed for our cantata. The choir is performing at
the six o'clock service on Christmas Eve."

"If you're hinting for me to join, I haven't set foot in a
church in years."

He'd attended as a child, since Mr. Lenny had served at
the local church as an associate pastor, but Max had gotten
away from anything religious once he heard of Mr. Lenny's
death. None of his other foster families, nor his birth mother,
had favored religion.

"Come once to rehearsal, Max, and see if you're a decent
fit. I think you are, though it's your call. The choir members
are good people and—"

"No one's refuting their goodness."

"Then help us out." Gerry extended a sheepish smile.

"Isn't Ryan Edwards your main singer?"

"Normally, although he's conducting the choir on Christmas Eve. And right now, he's in Atlanta rehearsing. Another member is stepping in for the next couple of weeks."

Max hesitated, ready to cut off any additional arguments from Gerry with a shake of his head.

"You're here for Christmas, correct?" Gerry asked. "And staying through New Year's."

"I am. However—"

"You'll recognize the traditional hymns: 'Away in a Manger,' etc. You'll catch on quick. You're a fine note-reader."

Max's eyebrows furrowed. His friend knew he wasn't a churchgoer, yet he was asking him to sing in a church choir. He considered Gerry's earnest expression as his mind scrambled for an excuse. At a loss for how to decline, he returned to the computer files.

"Did I mention Sarah is usually at the church when we rehearse?" Gerry added. "She designs and arranges the altar flowers. Sure looks pretty all decked out in red with green velvet ribbons."

"The church or your great-niece?"

Gerry winked. "Both."

Max sprang to his feet. "When are the rehearsals?"

"Thursday evenings at seven o'clock."

"Sarah is usually there?"

"Usually."

"I'll give the choir a try."

"I thought so." Gerry sent Max a knowing grin. "Oh, and bring your harmonica."

"Why?"

"The finale is a rousing rendition of 'We Wish You A

Merry Christmas.' I'm playing guitar and a harmonica would be a nice touch."

"What about Joseph Slater? He's a professional guitarist."

"He and his wife, Scarlett, are flying to Australia next week for a worship conference. They asked me to step in."

"No one else plays harmonica in this town?"

"None that I know of. Consider it an honor to be asked. I wanted to add a sixteen-measure solo at the end."

Max digested this and considered reverting to his earlier decision. Singing in the choir was one thing. Playing the harmonica in front of Ryan Edwards, a world-renowned opera singer, was quite another. He opened his mouth, but Gerry interrupted.

"The other day, Sarah mentioned hanging wreaths on all the church windows on Thursday night."

Max chuckled. "I'll bring my harmonica."

Gerry drained his cup. "I knew you wouldn't let the baritone section down."

CHAPTER FIVE

*H*armonica tucked in his pocket, and his favorite bow tie in place, Max arrived at the white-painted Memorial Street Church on Thursday evening. Night had darkened the winter sky, forming a blanket of black velvet, and the steeple soared proud and magnificent against it.

An outdoor nativity scene took center stage. The life-size creche included the Holy Family, two white lambs, kings and shepherds, and a wooden stable.

Gas street lamps were wrapped in fragrant pine boughs, and a trembling wind rustled the tree branches.

Inside, an assemblage of youthful and older men and women were taking their places on the risers, and a small group of women hung wreaths on the arched church windows.

Looking around, he spotted Sarah balanced on the third rung of a stepladder.

He strode over to her and tapped her on the back. "Good evening, Sarah."

She whirled and almost fell into his arms. A burst of

delight lit her face, and everything around him—the stained glass depicting Bible scenes, the whiffs of incense and candles, the other people's voices—faded away. The intensity of her gaze did funny things to his insides. Regardless of the way their last time together had ended, she looked pleased to see him.

"Max!" She clung to the sides of the ladder for support. "I chatted with my uncle Gerry this week and he claimed you're singing in the church choir."

"Temporarily," Max corrected.

"You're also in a band with him?"

"The Bearded Elves." Max steadied the ladder as she climbed down.

"The Bearded Elves? That's ... different."

"Don't get hung up on the name. It will change soon."

She tilted her head to the side.

"When you're *not* a number one hit band, you're granted some flexibility." He grinned. "Wait until February. You'll see."

But then, he wouldn't be here in February, which left him with a sense of sadness.

She didn't reply, accepting his explanation without question, not even with the prompt of "What happens in February?"

Then again, maybe she hadn't heard him.

"Uncle Gerry raved about your superb baritone voice and perfect pitch," she said instead.

"He's biased since he was an undergrad student in my bird-watching class." Max removed his jacket and placed it on a pew. "Besides, doesn't every choir member sing in tune?"

"I'm not certain. Based on my great-uncle's comments, some don't." Sarah stepped to a side table and gathered red spray roses and luxuriant ivy, creating an elegant bouquet in a green glass vase. "The choir is all volunteer. These folks aren't professional except for Ryan Edwards and a few of the others."

Max turned her to face him. "Are you brave, Sarah?"

She looked startled by his unexpected question. "I try."

"You're the most courageous woman I've ever known."

Her cheeks pinkened. "Thanks."

"I intend to explore Crandall's Mountain next weekend. Will you join me? I hesitated inviting you, considering our adventure last week."

"You mean, because of the bear?"

"Because of me. I apologize for my rudeness. We didn't part on the finest note."

"You're here now. The present is all that matters."

"Is that a yes?"

Her nod of affirmation was accompanied by a smile of delight. "Let me check my work schedule, but it sounds like fun."

She was full of life. Eager. Forgiving. And stunning. The hiking gear she'd worn the previous weekend hadn't done her justice. She'd looked anything but glamorous in a hooded jacket, snowflake gloves and boots. The woman gazing at him now was entrancing. By the light of numerous church candles, the jeweled sparkle of her emerald eyes mesmerized him.

"For the record, I like hiking more than ever," she said.

Her statement thrilled him, sending a rush of gladness straight to his heart.

Before he could reply, Gerry called him to the choir to begin the warm-up.

Max nodded at Gerry over his shoulder, then curved back to Sarah. "The rehearsal runs an hour. Will you be here when it's finished?"

"Most likely. There are thirty windows in the church."

"I'll see you after rehearsal then?"

She chewed her lip. Glanced away.

He stared at her in eager silence. "Well?"

"Sure. If I'm done beforehand, I'll wait."

The recognizable first notes of 'Joy To The World' led by the sopranos, announced the beginning of choir practice.

Max hurried to the risers and took his appointed place between Gerry and a gray-bearded man. He retrieved a hymnal and thumbed through the selections until he located the correct piece.

The uplifting lyrics and melody, published by Handel in the 1700s, plucked him backward to a tiny church, sitting on a hard wooden pew as he listened to Mr. Lenny's heartfelt sermon.

Max focused on the associate conductor for the most part during the rehearsal.

However, he often stole glances at Sarah. She wore black slacks and a shimmery candy-red sweater, and her slim figure kept drawing his attention.

Whenever she caught his gaze, she quickly looked away. However, she smiled first, and he reciprocated with a responsive grin.

The final selection called for a guitar and harmonica. The "honor" of playing a harmonica solo in front of the other musicians was one that Max would've happily forgone, but when he was done, he was satisfied with his performance.

"What's your decision?" Gerry asked once the rehearsal ended.

Max slid the harmonica into his pocket. "I'll join."

"What was the deciding factor? The beloved hymns, my brilliant persuasion, or my great-niece's presence?"

"The latter," Max assured him.

In a refined southern drawl, an elderly woman introduced herself as Mrs. Marge Addyson. Her gray hair was neatly coiffed, and her rouged cheeks plumped with her smile as she held out a freckled hand. "Your baritone voice is as fine as a sunny winter's day. Welcome to Cherish. I'm the associate pastor."

"Thank you, ma'am. I'm Maxwell Archer." He shook her hand, frail yet sturdy. He was surprised at the callouses.

In a deafening stage whisper that garnered the notice of the remaining choir members, Marge announced, "You're the professor birdman who went hiking with our Sarah."

Our Sarah?

Intent on sidestepping a discussion involving Sarah that might be overheard, Max replied, "I'm affiliated with an ornithology department at a university."

"Birds."

"Ornithology is a branch of zoology," he clarified, "and is a discipline involving the study of birds."

"Impressive, and a distinctive description."

"Animals are important in my life and profession."

He expected Marge to rhapsodize about the significance of pets. She did just that, but offered a particular recommendation.

"Nicholas, the town sheriff, is looking for someone to adopt a cuddly homeless puppy," Marge said. "Considering your animal expertise, you're ideal."

Although both startled and pleased by her consideration of him as a candidate, he replied, "I've already been asked by the woman who owns the music store."

"Dorothy Edwards?"

"Yes, and I declined."

"Aren't you a fan of stray mongrels?"

"I should be, because I'm one myself." He regarded her with an ironic grin. "I used to live in Cherish."

"When?"

"Three decades ago, and for a brief spell. My foster family's last name was Monroe."

"I don't recall a Monroe family, although oftentimes my

memory fails me." She pursed her lips. "I'll remember something that happened a decade earlier and forget something that happened a minute ago."

By the looks of Marge Addyson's well-heeled style and demeanor, Max assumed she resided in the wealthy outskirts of town. The Monroe family had occupied the impoverished fringes.

"I'm in no position to take on the responsibility of a dog," he said. "I move around a lot and my three parakeets are a literal handful. In January, I begin my dream job in Florida. I've struggled for ages to be on the faculty of a prestigious university."

"I express the feelings of the entire town when I say I'm overjoyed you're in Cherish." Marge reached for her handbag and tugged on a pair of flowered red gloves. "Regardless of your job, I hope you're here a long, long time."

"I appreciate your hospitality."

It warmed him—this undeniable sense of community, a welcome transition from big city living.

"Our church holds services on Saturday afternoons and Sunday mornings. On Christmas Eve day and evening, we offer several services." She studied him with an astute gaze. "Christmas is an opportune season to honor our Lord."

For a split second, their exchange grew awkward. Max wasn't about to divulge his lack of faith to the elderly associate pastor in the middle of a church.

He opted not to reply, although he recognized the wisdom flowing from her heart.

"You need honest and caring people in your life," she said.

He managed a grim smile.

"Do you serve God?"

Surprised at her bluntness, he answered truthfully. "I tried the religion route when I was younger. It didn't go well. The people in my circle ..." He shrugged.

"Perhaps the season has come for a different circle." She squeezed his hand, her intelligent eyes exuding care and friendship. "Press on, Max. We're all here for you in your journey."

Journey to where?

"'Thanks be to God for his indescribable gift,'" she proclaimed.

"Second Corinthians 9:15." At her lifted eyebrows and inquisitive gaze, he avoided eye contact. "My special foster father was a pastor," he said.

"Special?"

"Yes."

"Was?" She grasped her blue tweed coat draped over a music stand.

"Mr. Lenny died many years ago."

She fiddled with the silver bell brooch on her coat's lapel as she studied him. "You miss him."

"Very much." Max glanced toward Gerry, who was collecting choral music.

Gerry picked up his guitar, slicked back his white hair, and approached them. "Hi, Mrs. Addyson."

"Hello, Gerry." Marge smiled up at him. "I just asked our newest choir member if he was interested in adopting the stray pup that wandered into Nicholas's office."

"What was his answer?"

"I'm right here, Gerry." Because they were close friends, Max caught the drollness in Gerry's tone. "As much as I'd love a puppy, I can't commit."

"I refused as well because my plate is full. Sorry." Gerry flashed a guilt-ridden smile. "However, let's all go out for a celebratory drink at The Garden Terrace."

"What are we celebrating?" Max inquired.

"You joined the church choir."

"Don't you have to rush home to your new baby?" Caught

between amusement and confusion, Max and Marge inquired in unison.

Gerry shot them a look filled with emotions—including self-reproach and longing. "My mother-in-law is visiting and insisted on rocking the baby to sleep. She holds the magic touch."

Max grinned. "Therefore, your and your wife's roles aren't egalitarian tonight?"

"Little Freddie giggles from head to toe whenever I make faces at him," Gerry replied. "Or raspberry kisses. I'll do both in the morning."

Mrs. Addyson left shortly afterwards, pleading tiredness, and shaking her head in refusal at the invitation. She reminded them that she was past retirement age and went to bed early.

A bang of the ornately carved doors signaled the last of the choir members filing out.

Max peered around. Sarah was hanging a final wreath on a window.

"Go ahead to the restaurant," he instructed Gerry. "We'll be along shortly."

"We?"

"I'm hoping Sarah will join us."

Gerry clapped a hand on Max's back. "I'm rooting for you, my friend. I'll inquire about a gig at the restaurant while I'm waiting."

"Do you think the management will agree?"

"Simple logic. We order a meal and they'll hire our band."

"Just because we eat there doesn't mean they'll want us to *play* there," Max countered. "Hundreds of customers dine at the restaurant every day."

"It's a start."

"Will we get paid?"

"I was thinking more along the lines of free drinks."

Max bit back a grin at the logic he didn't see at all, pulled on his jacket and hurried to Sarah.

"Perfect timing," he declared.

"For what?"

"You're finished, and I am too."

"I'm *nearly* done." She swerved around him to a table and secured buckthorn berry branches into florist foam, then arranged the branches with a trail of ivy in a copper vase.

He followed her as she set the vase near the altar. "Will you join us?" he asked.

"Where?"

"The Garden Terrace."

"It's after eight o'clock."

"Hardly late."

"There's cleanup here. In addition, I'm scheduled for a double shift tomorrow."

"I'll finish." To Max's relief, a short, heavyset woman spoke up. "Sarah, you go on and enjoy yourself with this handsome newcomer."

Max turned to her. "How do you know I'm a newcomer?"

"Cherish is a small community." The woman reached for the last two poinsettias. "Word travels fast."

"Thank you, Rosemary." Sarah's shoulders lifted as she turned to Max. "I'd like to, but—"

"Do you have any noteworthy plans on a Thursday night?"

"After I tend to my pets, I planned to catch up on some reading."

He persevered. "Did you drive here?"

"I walked. I don't live far."

"There's a chill in the air, Cinderella. Ride with me, and I guarantee you'll arrive home before midnight. Besides, I don't know where the restaurant is."

She laughed. "I'm certain you can find it without my help." In the flick of a few seconds, her mood had switched from indecision to humor, and it struck him that no matter her disposition, he appreciated her companionship.

"I have it on excellent authority you're the ideal guide," he said.

She gathered a half dozen stemmed red roses and placed them in a bucket filled with water. "From whom?"

"Me."

With a sideways smile, Sarah retrieved her jacket, then tucked her hand through his arm.

He couldn't help grinning as he escorted her out the wooden doors and down the church steps.

CHAPTER SIX

The Garden Terrace wasn't the restaurant Max imagined. Certainly, the Monroes hadn't been able to afford such luxuries as dining out.

He'd pictured a genteel garden, a sparkling fountain, and an abundance of plants. After all, the restaurant's name alluded to a *garden*.

Instead, he and Sarah were welcomed by lively waitresses, a boisterous clatter of dishes, and heavenly whiffs of mesquite smoked chicken. An oversized sign at the entrance stated in bold letters, "The holidays are for barbecue." Multicolored lights were strung from the ceiling and pine cones and faux red berries wound around rustic poles, accentuated by tan burlap. A keyboardist provided a background performance of "Carol of the Bells."

"This restaurant doesn't subscribe to minimalism," he joked.

"They're renowned for sugar-free lemon cake and sweet tea," Sarah told Max as he led her through the crowd and ushered her to a booth Gerry had claimed.

Somehow, Max remembered that about this restaurant.

He'd eaten a slice of the cake in his youth and had savored every bite. Another aspect of this appealing town were that things stayed the same. A time machine rewound to an era without the push and shove of big-city living.

"Sugar and sugar-free." Max helped her off with her jacket, tugged off his, and hung both on a coat hanger. "Isn't that a juxtaposition?"

"An oxymoron." Sarah teased him with a nudge. He noticed that she had watched his lips as he spoke. The restaurant was noisy and even he strained to hear their conversation. "Or rather, one cancels out the other. The calories in sugary tea—"

"Is a paradox," Gerry interrupted, indicating the guitar on his seat. He motioned them to sit across from him.

"Wrong," they contradicted him, which produced lots of laughter.

In the minutes between ordering and waiting for their meals—hot chocolate topped with marshmallows for Sarah, a slice of the sugar-free lemon cake and tea for Max, and a draft beer and two platters of French fries for Gerry—Max arrived at several important deductions.

First, Gerry wasn't, as Max earlier had presumed, merely a first-rate student, a talented musician, and a newbie father. Gerry was also candid and clever. While he inquired about Max's and Sarah's hiking adventure, he closely observed the way Max draped an arm around her shoulders.

And Sarah, with her delicate features and lilting voice, had a remarkable gift. She was charismatic, and she gave an enthusiastic account of the bear adventure, flavoring it with enough elements to engage Gerry. By doing so, she successfully avoided any reference to the kiss she and Max had shared.

Smiling at her wide-eyed gaze as she described the

babbling river, he felt inside him the stirring of a sentiment so remote, so foreign, he gasped in denial.

He was falling for her.

Not in the cards, he told himself. He was leaving in January.

Even so, the sentiment prompted him to curve a lock of shiny hair behind her ear. Her glittery gold star earrings winked back at him.

"You forgot our interruption by the teenagers," he said.

Her eyes glistened with laughter. "If they hadn't approached, we would still be ..."

"Kissing," he whispered in her ear and squeezed her shoulder, a gentle reminder in case she'd forgotten.

Oblivious to the direction of the conversation, Gerry pulled out his cellphone, concentrated on a text and frowned. "My wife," he muttered.

"Is little Freddie sleeping?" Max inquired.

"Almost." Gerry tried for a smile that said all was well, although he didn't entirely convince Max.

After their drinks and food were served, Gerry took a deep pull from his beer and set it down. "Incidentally, my friend, management agreed."

"To what?" Max handed him a bottle of ketchup and watched him smother the fries, then slid the platter to the middle of the table for all to share.

"To us performing here a couple Fridays from now." Gerry broke off a fry and chewed. "The Bearded Elves are back in business."

Max helped himself to an ample portion of fries after scarfing down his cake. He'd forgotten how much he liked lemon. "We weren't ever *in* business. Nonetheless, your news is exciting. Are they paying us?"

"Our gig is doubling as a debut audition and management is requesting familiar holiday tunes." A smile quirked Gerry's mouth. "I'll organize a playlist. We can rehearse separately, then together before our unveiling."

Sarah joined in with a chuckle. "Am I invited?"

"Absolutely. We'll perform in that far corner. There's even a dance floor." With his half-eaten fry, Gerry gestured to where the keyboardist played on a small stage.

Once their table was cleared, Gerry insisted on paying the bill, then peered at his phone and announced, "I'm heading home before my wife and her mother murder me."

"Did the baby wake up?" Max asked.

"The baby never went to sleep."

"No magic touch from your mother-in-law?"

"Our next option is to phone Merlin the Magician. Evidently, little Freddie is offended by the idea of sleeping."

Sarah surged up as quickly as Gerry did. "I should leave too." She peered at the restaurant's rustic wall clock, which showed after nine o'clock.

"Don't rush on my account." Gerry waved toward the dance floor. The keyboardist had begun a jazzy rendition of Ray Charles's "That Spirit of Christmas," and a handful of couples swirled to the rhythm.

Max slid his arm around Sarah and led her to the intimate dance floor. She was so petite, scarcely five feet tall, her head hardly reached his shoulder.

She gazed up at him with a jesting smile. "Are you the type who steps on your dance partner's feet?"

"Exactly." He chuckled, tempted to kiss the edges of her smile. "You?"

"The same, so watch out." Her laughter was mellow and melodic. He loved her ability to laugh at herself, as well as with him.

"Has anyone ever described you as a wonderful, caring man?" she asked.

"I dislike labels."

"I do too, but my intuition tells me you're a good person."

"Never tell a man he's good. Strong, maybe, or marvelous—"

She rested her head against his chest, and he whirled them around and around. Her steps were agile, gliding to the rhythm. Above them, the multi-colored lights sparkled, creating a wondrous, otherworldly effect. Her hair spun with each pivot and twist, and he kissed her forehead, her cheeks, her lips.

"What a wonderful feeling," he sang, adlibbing the lyrics, "to waltz with a precious, vivacious woman who is as sweet as a sugarplum."

As they danced, he reviewed the plan he'd conceived within the past half hour. While he lived in Cherish, he'd see her as often as possible.

Her descriptions of him—good and caring—were poignantly familiar. Mr. Lenny's wife had often called him a "caring little boy." Once, his outlook on life had shone optimistic.

His timeworn thoughts now were shadowed with the awareness that a future with a loving wife hadn't come to pass.

He blew out a labored breath.

He'd gotten over the injustice of being born to birth parents who couldn't focus on anyone except themselves.

Some children were born lucky. Other weren't.

But now he'd met Sarah.

How wonderful they could spend a few weeks together.

How awful they could only spend a few weeks together.

Seeming to sense the dipping of his mood, Sarah muttered she was sorry for stepping on his foot—she hadn't—but her comical expression portrayed her attempt to cheer him and her refreshing humor. But then she added, "I should get home."

With a nod, he maneuvered her off the dance floor and retrieved their jackets. Outside, the streets were dark and quiet. Gas lamps flickered, forming pools of warm light.

"How far do you live from the restaurant?" he asked.

"Three blocks." She turned right. "My house is in the center of town."

"I'll escort you. It'll give me a chance to walk off my fried-food coma."

Plus, it would take longer than a quick drive in his car, and he wanted to enjoy every precious minute with her. He pointed toward the town square as he heard voices rise in harmony. He recognized the "Silent Night" refrain.

"What's going on?" he asked.

Sarah hesitated. "Going on?"

"The singing."

"Oh, singing. It's carol singing," she replied. "The town's Christmas committee sponsors caroling three nights a week in December. Anyone can join. Afterwards, they serve hot apple cider and roasted chestnuts."

Now that she had mentioned it, he recognized the scorching charcoal aroma, rich and nutty, permeating the air, along with the hint of woodsy fireplaces.

Beams of silver fell around them. A full moon graced the sky, and a smattering of stars twinkled in shimmering beauty.

A chilly burst of wind tugged at their jackets.

Sarah bowed her head and closed her eyes to avoid the sting.

His gaze fell to her long, thick eyelashes, an unmistakable reddish-blond. Her copper-colored hair, as smooth as the finest silk, fell loose around her face.

"I recalled Carolina weather being warm all year round," he said, "but my remembrances are from a youngster's perspective."

"How long were you here?"

"Briefly." He shifted the subject, in no mood to upset the fine balance of a pleasant evening by being reminded of his tumultuous upbringing. "I assumed the climate was comparable to Florida."

"Do you like hot weather?"

"In all honesty, no." His reflective pause initiated a jab from his conscience. *Dream job, remember? You're moving.* "How about you?"

"I've lived here my entire life. I know everyone and am comfortable here. Still, I sometimes wish to see other places."

"Like Florida?"

"Are there more palm trees than the Carolinas?"

"Probably."

"You'll receive a pay raise with your new job?"

"Not necessarily, although I'm optimistic my research will resonate with people avid about ornithology. That is, unless my appointment is cancelled. Universities are tightening their proverbial belts, and bird study isn't at the top of their budgets." He shrugged, sighed. "If it happens, it happens."

"You work a lot of hours. It's a considerable workload." She seemed to choose her words carefully.

"Which will become heavier once I take on more responsibility."

"I'm sorry you're not a hot-weather fan."

"I don't particularly like cold weather, either. Nor do I care for synthetic snow, the kind the outdoor fairs manufacture for gala events."

"The Carolinas enjoy four distinct seasons," she replied. "I eagerly wait for snow on Christmas Day. No assurances, though. The weather here is unpredictable."

"I lived up north for years. If it doesn't snow, we're surprised."

She grinned. "In Cherish, if it *does* snow, we're amazed."

Several of the shops' single-paned windows had frosted

over, and they peered through the glass, admiring one-of-a-kind gifts—a man's handmade striped red tie, a vintage green and gold pinecone necklace, and jars touting themselves as a "One-Stop Spa." An innovative store advertised a pet-friendly dog bakery, and Sarah commented on the unique toys, ranging from whimsical Merry Christmas bandanas to tail-wagging elf sweaters.

While they strolled, she was more outgoing than the day of their hike, regaling him with hilarious stories of her pets, beginning with what happened when she returned from work each day to a houseful of welcoming animals.

"My two dogs and two cats wait by the door until I arrive," she described. "Even if I leave for ten minutes to get the mail at the post office, they're under the impression I've been gone for hours, and the greeting parade begins anew."

She grew more gorgeous by the second. Her cheeks had grown rosy from the cold, her wide-set eyes sparkling a deep emerald. When she chuckled, tiny puffs of her breathing filled the air. He couldn't look away.

"My budgies are happy," he said. "They spend their days singing or talking."

"Uncle Gerry told me they haven't mimicked the birdsongs you recorded."

"Nothing yet."

Max went over the endless hours he'd spent with his birds. Why wouldn't they mimic other birdsongs or harmonica music? He reined in his frustration and focused on Sarah. "My budgies have individual temperaments. One male is timid, the other bolder, and the third, a female, speaks her mind."

"Hurray for the female. What does she say?"

Max pushed out an exasperated breath. "'God bless us, every one.'"

"From *A Christmas Carol?* Tiny Tim?"

"Exactly. She's a rescue bird. An elderly woman owned her."

"What's her name?"

"Angel." He resisted the urge to laugh. "Don't be fooled. She's the most unangelic bird of the three."

"Is unangelic a word?"

"It is now."

"We all have distinctive personalities, because God created variety and uniqueness."

"You're saying He knew what to do."

"Exactly."

"But how, Sarah? I'm not at peace with all this religious jargon."

"Don't search for peace." Her tone softened, and he felt his expression grow less rigid. "You already are at peace. God is inside you."

She expressed herself with her body, gestures, and expressions rather than a deluge of words.

He had appreciated her artistic flower arrangements at church and he knew she was hard working and industrious. Her faith in God was clear, and he sensed she possessed what Mr. Lenny had called "a new creature in Christ." Combined, these attributes contributed to her magnetic personality.

In the sparkle of twinkling lights dancing from nearby homes, the sadness in his heart diminished. Sarah carried the same unique gift—to enhance the world around her merely by her presence. She was an extraordinary, special woman.

Soon, they reached the gaily decorated Musically Yours. Although the music store was closed, they paused to admire the window display of the polar bears, treble clef signs, and model train.

How many hours, Sarah mused aloud, had it taken Dorothy and Ryan to dress up the window with such flair?

"Maybe they had help," Max said.

"From who? A polar bear?"

"Maybe Beethoven himself." Max curled his fingers around hers. Happiness lifted his spirits, and, judging by Sarah's contented sigh, the holiday atmosphere of the winsome town affected them both.

"Cherish Hills Inn also has particularly noticeable decorations. The inn is located farther up the street." Sarah gestured with her chin. "The innkeeper, Tom Canning, is a long-time resident, and strict about who he rents to."

"I tried to get a room there, but Tom wasn't keen on renting to me and my birds for the entire month of December."

"Not surprising. The inn is posh and unconducive for pets."

"Ah. That explains Tom's half-hearted response."

"What did he say?"

Max grabbed a mouthful of air and shouted, "No."

"That's why Tom doesn't have anyone currently staying at his inn. He's choosey and a stickler for elegance."

"Thank you." Max picked her up and twirled her around.

"What for?" She giggled. Wriggled.

"For sticking up for me."

"I did?"

"Yes. You stuck up for me instead of Tom."

"I'm getting dizzy. Put me down."

He continued to spin, but slower this time, holding her close. "Not until you guarantee me something."

"You expect an assurance after that?"

"Promise me you'll never change." He gazed at her amazing face, trying to ignore the flip in his pulse.

She met his stare. "Our lives, our paths, take many forms, Max."

He spoke clearly and deliberately, as he had done all evening. "Not with us."

He set her down and reached for her hand, whistling the entire last block to her house. It was set back from the road and surrounded by bare-branched trees. The front door was painted gray and bedecked with shiny pink ornaments and a garland heavy with silver tinsel.

"You're a true holiday-lover," he remarked. "I hope the porch doesn't collapse under the sheer mass of the decorations."

At her doorstep, with barking dogs and loud meows in the background, he slipped his arms around her. So close their foreheads touched, he tipped up her chin and kissed her.

She stood on her tiptoes and yielded to his hungry mouth. Her lips were plump and inviting, fitting together with his, two pieces of an intricate puzzle matching perfectly. Her hands reached up and her slim fingers tangled behind his neck.

Her enticing sweetness obliterated his concerns—an uncertain job market, his research, his turbulent past—and he savored every second of their kiss. The promise of December, creamy hot chocolate and tart lemon cake—he'd hit the jackpot when he met Sarah.

He was filled with anticipation and gladness.

And a spark that completely surprised him.

A spark of love.

CHAPTER SEVEN

*T*he following day, Sarah clocked in at the greenhouse at ten o'clock in the morning. Fragrant whiffs of lush evergreens never failed to bring thoughts of sparkly white lights and an array of gaily wrapped gifts.

That morning, she'd secured her flyaway hair with a green headband because it always frizzed after shampooing, even when she used her favorite rosewood shampoo. Then, she'd tugged on a cream-colored cable-knit sweater, jeans, and snowman dangle earrings.

After a wave at Bonnie, who had positioned herself at the cash register, Sarah sorted Christmas cactus. She lavished care on each showy red and white flower. Many had been overwatered, which led to root and stem rot.

While she tended to the first plant, she tried to ignore the butterflies in her chest as memories of her previous evening with Max kept surfacing.

His animated features when he chatted about his birds, his quick-witted banter, his musicality, were all part of his personality. He was bold yet vulnerable; humorous yet sensitive.

And she loved every minute she spent with him.

He'd dismissed his upcoming Florida job with a casual "if it happens, it happens" as he rubbed the dark stubble of his beard. Nonetheless, his dismissal had only confirmed that he cared about the prestigious position more than he let on.

The plants, she reminded herself. The plants.

She tended to the next one and again, her mind meandered.

The mouth-watering food and drink at The Garden Terrace, her intimate dance with Max, their leisurely stroll ending in an earth-shattering kiss—all those memories came back in a rush. Rational thought had a way of abandoning her whenever she was within two feet of him.

She pressed a finger to her lips. Was last night a first date? After all, he'd invited her to a restaurant. Or was it a second if she counted their hike on Juniper Mountain?

"Do you have any noteworthy plans on a Thursday night?" he'd asked her.

Um, no, unless scrubbing the kitchen floor and vacuuming were considered noteworthy. In any event, she was glad she'd accepted his invitation.

At the end of the evening, he'd requested her phone number and had promised to text, phone, and see her often.

He was a man, he assured her, who never reneged on his promises. True to his word, he'd texted a few minutes later, telling her how much he'd enjoyed their hours together. That text had resulted in an hour's worth of conversation.

Was his kiss the beginning of something extraordinary, something lasting?

As quickly as it came, she released the thought.

He was in Cherish for one month. He'd made that fact abundantly clear.

Nevertheless, his affectionate words and tender actions were sincere.

Weren't they? What if he didn't call or text again?

A favorite passage from the Bible, Matthew 6:34, reassured her: "Do not be anxious for tomorrow, for tomorrow will be anxious for itself."

She wondered about Max's past, because Marge Addyson had left a voice mail for Sarah that morning when Sarah was in the shower.

"I scoured the Big Brothers Big Sisters files," Marge said. "I believe I've found a photo of your Max, probably taken close to thirty years ago when he lived in Cherish with his foster family. You'll want to see it, I'm sure. I'll stop by your home ... I'm assuming after six o'clock? Call me if that's not okay."

Her Max.

Sarah's heartbeat had drummed at Marge's reference, and she scarcely paid attention to the rest of Marge's words.

Wait.

Big Brothers Big Sisters.

Despite Max's brilliant mind and academic demeanor, his background apparently wasn't silver-spoon. She considered him handsome, but there was a blunt masculinity to his square jaw and muscled physique. Had he been the type of boy who'd been in many brawls?

She knew he wasn't afraid of anything.

Not even a charging bear.

By the river, his strong, chiseled arms had held her tight.

Images of a Christmas spent with him brought comfort to her lonely world, a breathlessness whenever she recalled the glimmer of interest in his gray eyes. His dark hair, a tad too long, curled at the nape, and she'd wanted to smooth the adorable cleft on his chin.

By far, he was the handsomest man to set foot in Cherish.

He's leaving, her sensible side was quick to remind. *Do you honestly want to get hurt again?*

A jarring announcement over the store's loudspeaker called for a price check. Quickly yanked back to the present, Sarah surveyed the rows of cacti, trying to recall which plants she'd tended. White blooms or red?

The nursery door opened, and a blast of wintry air hit her.

Nicholas, the town sheriff, accompanied by Molly Belle, his rambunctious golden retriever, strode toward her. Molly Belle's leash didn't prevent her from romping away from him. She knocked over a bunch of plants in her hurry to chase … nothing.

"Stop." Nicholas tugged on the leash and peered at the spilled soil on the concrete floor. "Sorry, Sarah."

"It's a fast clean-up." Sarah grinned at Molly Belle. "Are those doggy obedience classes helping?"

Nicholas shoved a hand through his blond hair. "The instructor recommended she get lots of exercise. What an understatement." His moan was part sigh, part frustration. "We take her out often, although she's easily distracted."

The dog beamed up at them with expectant black eyes, then went back to lapping the water spilled from the plants.

"Here, Molly Belle." Sarah grabbed a water bottle, foraged for an empty container, and poured water into it. "You'll find this is tastier."

Nicholas crossed his arms and turned to face her. "You're one of only a handful of people Molly Belle will listen to."

Sarah appreciated that aspect of living in a small community. Folks were now using strong, clear voices when talking to her. Needless to say, it wasn't because she had a hearing impairment, despite what her friends hinted. They merely needed to speak louder, especially when she was in a crowded place with many voices.

Perhaps another reason why Dorothy had recommended Sarah as Max's hiking companion was because she knew that Sarah preferred the quiet solitude of nature.

"Molly Belle isn't obeying your commands?" she teasingly asked Nicholas.

"Once in a while. Once in a *great* while."

Sarah laughed, wiped her hands on her employee apron, and grabbed a broom. "Are you purchasing anything in particular today?"

"I'm here for two reasons. First, my wife wants a live wreath for the front door, rather than the fake one I purchased at the grocery store."

"The wreaths are all hung outside. You passed them when you entered." Sarah swept the soil into the dustpan and discarded it. "What's the second reason?"

"I hoped to discuss the puppy who wandered into the sheriff's office—"

"We discussed the subject. My answer is no."

"Sarah, you're the ideal choice."

"I can't, Nicholas. My house is overrun with pets."

He kneaded the back of his neck. "You have two cats and a hamster."

"Plus two dogs."

"Your dogs are friendly."

"You didn't remember I owned dogs until a second ago. My Shih Tzu is ten years old and set in her ways, and the other dog is a cocker spaniel who thinks she owns me rather than the other way around. I'm confident someone will welcome the puppy as the perfect addition to their family."

"Who?" Nicholas muttered, half to himself. He tugged his phone from his pocket, scrolled through it, then drew her attention to a tiny puppy with fuzzy silver-colored fur. "Do you agree he needs a loving home for Christmas?"

"Absolutely." She scrutinized the photo. "He?"

"Yup." Nicholas eyed Molly Belle, who had secured a place on the concrete floor in a spot of sunshine. "He lacks a safe, loving environment. Here's some videos. Doesn't he look like he's ready to take on the world?"

A bouncy puppy filled the screen, a roll of fat evident under his chin. In the second video, he chased Nicholas and nipped at his pant legs. This was followed by a short bark as the puppy rolled onto his back and stared into the camera with sweet doggy eyes.

"We've had him vet checked and he's healthy. Plus, he's handled daily and exhibits a devoted personality." Nicholas pointed to the screen. "Look at that shiny coat."

"That puppy is in constant motion. Wagging his tail and wriggling all over the place."

"He's a gem, right? The vet estimated he's eight weeks old, and vaccinated him for the first series of shots."

Sarah smiled and leaned in. "Nicholas, you're persuasive, but—"

A tap on the shoulder caused her to whirl.

"Hi, Sarah." Max stepped within a foot of her. He smiled at her and scowled at Nicholas. "Am I interrupting something?"

"Max." She touched her fingers to her throat. "I didn't expect to see you today."

He shoved his hands in his pockets. His lips pressed together. "I wanted to say hello and—"

He looked sinfully handsome, and the thought crossed her mind that Nicholas might book Max, because it had to be illegal to be that good-looking. He wore black jeans that accented his toned legs and a chambray shirt. His familiar bow tie peeked beneath the olive-green twill jacket.

The time showed mid-morning—the hours when Max normally pored over research.

Yet, he was here, and her heart did a slow flip.

Max's scowl stayed on Nicholas.

"You're not interrupting a thing." Nicholas clicked his phone shut and shoved it back in his pocket.

Sarah flinched, sensing an unmistakable hostility between the two men.

"I'm glad you stopped by the store, Max." She gave an uneasy laugh and swallowed. "Let me introduce you to the Cherish town sheriff. Nicholas Thompson, meet Maxwell Archer."

At the same height, six feet tall, both men's features were similar—sharp and athletic and wary.

They shook hands, although Max treated Nicholas with chilly courtesy. He bent to pet Molly Belle. She responded with a gleeful tail wag.

"I'm Dorothy Edwards's brother," Nicholas clarified as Max straightened. "My wife, Emmanuelle, teaches harp lessons at Dorothy's store."

Max's expression eased. "You're off duty today, sheriff?" He sized up Nicholas' casual attire of khakis and a sweater, then positioned himself between Sarah and Nicholas, bracing a hand on a pole above her head. Although the men's verbal volley might have ended, Max was sending Nicholas a clear message.

He was interested in Sarah.

Because he was jealous. Jealous of *her*. The knowledge brought a wry smile.

"Nice bow tie," Nicholas said flatly.

"Thanks."

Okay, so it was unusual to wear a bow tie into a garden center, but Max was unique. The tie made him unforgettable, offering an air of distinguished academia. Although, considering his disheveled hair, he reminded her of an absent-minded professor.

"Today is my day off." Nicholas offered a scarcely

disguised smirk. "You don't, by any wild chance, break the law, Max, do you?"

"Never, sheriff. I'm new in town, and my rental is begging for a little holiday cheer." His gaze rested on Sarah. "I'm here to purchase flowers. Can you help me, Sarah?"

"Definitely."

"Dorothy mentioned our little town had acquired another fine musician," Nicholas said. "The other day, a man stopped by her store to buy a harmonica. I assume that was you?"

"I'm an average musician and a temporary resident," Max corrected.

Nicholas narrowed his gaze. "So, you're here *temporarily*."

"Yes."

Nicholas glanced at the pole where Max still braced his arm. "You won't want to get too familiar with folks, then, if you're leaving them soon." With a crisp nod, he turned toward the entrance. "Well, I'm off to grab a wreath. C'mon, Molly Belle."

The dog didn't move and stared up at Nicholas with a kindly expression.

"Come." Gently, Nicholas pulled the leash.

Again, no response.

"Up, Molly Belle." Sarah ducked beneath Max's arm and stepped over to the sunny spot where the dog sat. "Up Molly Belle. Obey your master."

Molly Belle immediately stood. Her tail wagged with so much enthusiasm her entire body shook.

"You do have a way with animals, Sarah." Nicholas extended a rueful laugh, then regarded Max. "Don't forget that she's an exceptional woman, and well-loved by everyone in this town."

Max gave Sarah a teasing wink. "I've already discovered she's extraordinary, and she's hands down the bravest woman I've ever known."

Sarah felt her cheeks flush pink. She blamed it on the heat and sun in the garden center.

As Nicholas and Molly Belle headed out the door, she set down the broom she hadn't realized she still held. "What types of plants are you looking for, Max?"

"My birds are happiest around dazzling flowers."

"The poinsettias this year are brilliant." She signaled for him to follow her. "Any particular shade?"

After he selected two vibrant red poinsettias and a purple cyclamen with upswept flowers and silver foliage, he said, "A bike was left in my rental and I rode it here. Any chance you can bring the plants by my house when you get off work?"

"I'm done at six o'clock."

He nodded. "Excellent. I'll prepare dinner for us."

"I can't." She bent to pick up Molly Belle's water dish. "I haven't decorated the inside of my house for Christmas and I planned to start hauling decorations down from the attic tonight. Although I don't know why I do both inside and outside decorating. The cats think the artificial tree is a scratching post, and the dogs chew the ornaments. And don't get me started on holiday baking. Why, the dogs will eat everything in sight and ..."

She was babbling, and Max was grinning.

"Can decorating wait one more day?" he asked.

Something in his tone prompted her to study him.

A couple of customers wandered over, asking how to care for a Christmas cactus.

"My specialty," Sarah exclaimed. She cut her conversation with Max short and bustled over to show them the array of cacti. When they had chosen one and carried it to the register, Max was standing exactly where she'd left him.

She intended to refuse his invitation, but an entirely different answer emerged from her lips. "I need to stop home first."

"No problem. Say, seven o'clock?" His expression had softened. He looked pleased.

"You cook?"

"No. Fortunately, The Garden Terrace offers a delicious barbecue takeout."

"If you drive to the restaurant, you can easily swing to the nursery for your plants."

"Hmm." He shuffled his feet.

"Hmm?"

His gaze leveled on hers, the teasing evident. "I'll grant that your idea makes sense, although it ruins my excuse."

"Which is?"

"To see you tonight."

A giggle escaped her. "It would be a true calamity if your excuse was ruined."

"Is your answer a yes?"

"I'd love to have dinner with you."

Her spirits soared madly beneath the brilliance of his ready smile.

CHAPTER EIGHT

*A*nother December night had fallen in the Carolinas, and stars emerged in the sky one by one.

When Max ushered Sarah inside his slightly messy bunga-low, she immediately noticed the three colorful blue, white and green budgies near the window—two sharing one cage, the other alone in a separate cage. Mounds of scientific and bird magazines were stacked on a desk, the floor, and various shelves.

He kissed her tenderly on the cheek, thanked her for delivering the flowers, and rushed to take her coat. "Come. Sit on the sofa. It's comfortable. I made chip and dip."

Although he set the poinsettias and cyclamen on a tall pedestal table, she felt his probing silver gaze drift over her.

"I bought sandwiches, slaw, and a gingerbread cake for dessert." He gestured to the kitchen beyond. "Homemade wassail is simmering in the crock pot."

The cinnamon and apple aroma of the wassail made her mouth water. She grabbed a chip.

"I assumed you didn't cook," she said.

"I don't, but this is an easy family recipe."

Ah, so he had a family. When the subject had come up while they'd texted the night before, he'd veered to other topics—the weather, his research, his birds.

"Well, it smells delicious." She skimmed her fingers across her brown leather tote bag, which contained a precious manila envelope. When she'd stopped home after work to feed her animals and change into dark-wash jeans and a red striped sweater, Marge Addyson had met her at the door.

"Here is the photo from Big Brothers Big Sisters. Max looks young." Marge pressed the sealed manila envelope into Sarah's hands with excessive care. "He's very sweet and that worries me."

"Then or now?"

"Both. That sweet boy has become a charming, caring man."

"Why are you worried?"

"At choir rehearsal I stood across from him, and he could hardly keep his eyes off you. I wasn't sure the interest was mutual, but then I saw your return smiles. He cares for you a great deal."

"We've been friends only a short time," Sarah reminded Marge.

"But long enough. I know you, Sarah, and there's not a mean bone in your body. Do you believe in love at first sight?"

"Is there such a thing?"

"Certainly." Marge paused. "Max tries to hide it, but he's wearing his heart on his sleeve. I was at The Garden Terrace this afternoon for a bit of tea and cake, and he was there, ordering dinner for the two of you. He drove everyone crazy, asking about your favorite foods, obsessing about creating a splendid meal. It was almost as if the queen of England was coming to dine. He insisted on an exceptional holiday dessert."

"Lemon cake?"

"Gingerbread."

"He is very sweet." Sarah offered an affable grin, the kind that pacified fussy customers. Nonetheless, Marge wasn't easily placated.

"And?" Marge asked.

"I care for him a great deal too," Sarah replied. "However, he's leaving in January."

"Is he?"

"A promising career opportunity awaits him in Jacksonville. He's looking forward to it."

"Uh huh." Marge nodded perceptively. "Remember the Bible verse from Corinthians? 13:13?"

Sarah recited along with Marge. "And now these three remain: faith, hope, and love. But the greatest of these is love."

*N*ow, standing in Max's living room, Sarah adjusted her leather tote bag.

"I finished another page of my research paper a few minutes ago," he was saying "This timing worked out well. Dinner at seven is an ideal fit for me."

"Me too."

"Do you often eat alone?" he asked.

"More often than not. You?"

"It depends." He exhaled. "Who am I kidding? I always eat alone." He ran his thumb and forefinger along the edge of a laptop computer, then firmly closed it. "Would you like to meet my uncooperative birds?"

She chuckled. "Sure."

"I want to tell you, Sarah, I'm thrilled you're here."

The question in his persuasive gray eyes was well-defined. *Do you feel the same?*

Slightly, she bobbed her head, a silent response he immediately understood.

He took her in his arms and kissed her. Long and sweet. Her eyes closed, and her breath came in a sigh. He kissed her again and again. Deeply, exquisitely, and soundly.

After the kisses, with her head against his chest, Sarah smiled. Things were so good.

But only for now.

She lived in Cherish, worked at a job she enjoyed, and embraced her church, family and friends. He was off to a promising career opportunity in Jacksonville.

She was a Christian.

He was not.

She loved Christmas.

He tolerated Christmas.

Therefore, she must steel herself for their imminent separation.

She pulled out of his arms, brushed a hand over her hair, which she'd secured in a French braid, and approached the bird cages.

The parakeets squawked as she peered inside.

"Hello, pretty birds," she said.

All three began chirping at once. Vibrant birdsongs flooded the room.

Max came beside her, looping an arm around her. "Fascinating," he said, staring at the birds.

"What's fascinating?"

"The birds. Their reaction to you. I've never seen such behavior from them before."

*L*ater, they dined in his tiny kitchen on scrumptious barbecue served on his finest white ceramic plates, drinking bottled water. When dinner was finished, he ushered her into the living room and switched on the overhead pendant light.

"Would you like a mug of my homemade wassail with our dessert?" he asked. "The gingerbread is from the restaurant."

"You didn't make the gingerbread too?" she joked.

"My contribution to a festive meal is wassail." He retreated to the kitchen, then returned with two steaming mugs of wassail and slices of gingerbread on a tray. The consummate host. He set the tray on the coffee table, handed her a mug, and took the other for himself. He tapped a seat beside him on the sofa, waited for her to sit, then settled so close their legs touched.

She sniffed appreciatively. Fruity, spicy aromas rising from the mug conjured images of Christmas. The perfect warm drink for a brisk winter night.

She happily sipped and nibbled. The gingerbread tasted fresh out of the oven—sugary, buttery, and delectable. She expressed her compliments aloud, then added, "You touched on the fact that wassail is a family recipe."

Max smiled, but it was distant and distracted. His forehead tensed, and he gave the impression of wrestling with her statement.

Into the beat of an uncomfortable silence, she said, "I have a surprise for you from Big Brothers Big Sisters. Marge Addyson came by my house." Sarah drew the envelope from her tote bag. "She brought this."

Max frowned and pushed his plate of half-eaten gingerbread to the side. "Which is?"

She noted the hesitation in his voice and dipped her head toward the envelope. "A photo of you when you lived in Cherish. You were ... maybe twelve years old?"

He faltered. "Close enough."

"You attended Big Brothers, correct?"

"Every afternoon after school when the Monroes worked late." He managed a sardonic laugh. "Or rather, when they forgot about me, which was often."

Knowing she might be placing him in an awkward situation, she handed him the envelope with the same care as Marge had handed it to her.

"You don't have to open it if you don't want to," Sarah said.

"I'd like to." Yet he flinched, as if gearing for a disappointment.

He shoved out a breath, then withdrew a black-and-white glossy photograph.

Sarah peered over his shoulder. "Is that you?"

He nodded. The dark-haired boy staring back at them held a stoic expression. His fingers grasped the collar of an enormous dog who stood by his side.

Her heart turned over at the boy's brave demeanor, despite the uncertainty in his eyes. She wanted to hug the photo to her chest, hug the young boy and never let him go.

"Your features haven't changed." Emotions welled inside her, although she managed to keep her tone even. "I'd recognize you anywhere with that determined expression. It's been what, over thirty years?"

Max sipped his wassail, a deceptively casual gesture. "I remember when this was taken, right around Christmas."

"Is that your dog?"

"Not mine. The Monroes." His gaze swung to the parakeets, who perched silently on their swings. "I missed that dog more than anything when I was moved to another foster family. More than I missed the Monroes. Much more."

Sarah swallowed the lump in her throat. "What type of breed was the dog?"

"A Labrador husky." Max rubbed his eyes with his forefinger.

She waited for him to continue, but he showed every sign of being lost in troubled reflections. He stared at the photo, then looked away.

"What was the dog's name?"

"Tinsel."

She studied the photo. A young Max stood outside Big Brothers Big Sisters. His jeans were five inches too short for his long legs. He looked thin, almost undernourished. But his eyes were warm. Max's eyes.

"Want me to refresh your wassail?" he asked.

"I'm good, thanks." She held a hand over her mug. "Did you want to discuss the photo?"

"Nope. I'm a foster kid, Sarah. I moved around a lot. I had some good foster parents, and some not so good." He choked on the words. "The Monroes were not so good."

"And the family where you learned to make wassail?"

"Mr. Lenny's family."

"Where are they now?"

"He and his wife died. My foster brother, John, lives in Portugal. A few years ago, I gave up trying to stay in touch with him."

"Why?"

"What's the point? He lives so far away." Max didn't move a muscle. He cleared his throat. "Do you suppose it's in a man's best interest to suppress unhappy events, to keep them hidden from the woman he's falling in love with?"

Sarah's cheeks warmed. *Max was talking about her.* "The question is, how can that woman help a man repair those inner hurts?"

"I don't know. Sometimes I want relief from all the past pain." His face was expressionless. "My heritage, or rather, lack of heritage."

Now she understood where his resolve to make something of himself had been formed. It had started with the photo.

Or perhaps years earlier. Perhaps in other photos, in different towns with different families. Perhaps with different pets. And every single heartbreaking situation had strengthened Max with the fortitude to break free and make something of himself.

"Try prayer," she said softly.

"Been there." He linked his hands behind his head and peered at the ceiling pendant. "Done that."

"Try again."

His memories, unwelcome and agonizing, would continue to haunt him until he released them.

He dragged in a breath. "Years ago, I prayed to God to grant my foster brother a successful surgery."

"Go on."

"John only got one shot at a basketball scholarship. I knew how much it meant to Mr. Lenny."

She measured her words. "What happened?"

"God didn't listen. A week before Christmas, John's last surgery left him with a distinct limp and one leg shorter than the other."

"A physical disability." Sarah slid her fingers through Max's. The appeal, the warmth of his hand ... this attraction only grew stronger each time they were together. "A handicap."

"Handicap? Ask John how much of a handicap. He didn't attend college. Now he lives in a faraway village, and I haven't seen him in years."

"How did Mr. Lenny react after the failed surgery? You obviously hold him in high esteem."

"He didn't share my anger and frustration at God. He was a pastor—a virtuous and noble man. After listening to my ranting, he reminded me that John was alive and healthy, which was all that mattered."

"Lenny was right."

"At what cost?" Max tore his hand from hers. "Why were the other athletes on John's team strong and whole? He had a promising pro basketball future."

"Lenny was a man of faith."

Max stared straight ahead. He didn't seem aware any longer that she sat beside him. "Lenny declared that John had God on his side and God was all he needed."

"You don't agree?"

"I can't shake my resentment toward a God who plays favorites."

"Try again. Try prayer," she repeated.

"Prayer will make the hurt go away?"

"God will. Reflect on the healing truths of His words every day."

Max lifted his arms and surveyed the room. "I don't see God anywhere."

"Just because you don't see Him, doesn't mean He isn't here."

His expression gradually relaxed, and her chest still ached for him. He had erected a barrier around his heart. A barrier that was impossible to breach until he put aside his resentment and anger.

Pushing up from the sofa, he carried himself stiffly as he walked to the computer.

A moment later, birdsongs floated through the room, the same songs he'd recorded during their hike.

She came to stand close and motioned to the parakeets. "They aren't repeating anything?"

"Nothing. Not even when I play my harmonica."

The single green and white budgie in a wrought iron cage flapped her elegant feathers. In a clear, bell-like voice, she said, "God bless us, every one."

CHAPTER NINE

A few hours later, Sarah headed home.

Max sat on his living room's threadbare carpet and leaned against the sofa.

She was exceptional, fascinating, and extraordinary. More than extraordinary.

The Big Brothers photo had transported him back to the land of unfulfilled dreams. Life with the Monroes had been intolerable, specifically during Max's difficult adolescence.

He wasn't certain why Marge Addyson had gone to the trouble to find that photo and then give it to Sarah. A woman of well-meaning honesty, she may have wanted him to confront past issues in order to move forward.

But he'd done that already, hadn't he? He was accomplished. He'd succeeded in establishing a noteworthy career. Besides, life-altering injustices could never be forgiven.

He shook his head, a rueful smile. His thoughts harbored the very bitterness he thought he'd overcome.

Days ago, Sarah had encouraged him to reflect on the truths of God's word.

"Start with Psalms," she had advised. "The verses will promote healing, comfort and well-being."

"All that?" he questioned.

"All that," she echoed an assurance.

He'd heeded her advice about reading the Bible, although he hadn't told her. It wasn't a subject that came up in daily conversation. Although he could have told her tonight ...

Sarah. Sarah. Sarah. They were friends, and there were times when she kept him at arms-length. But there were other times when an electrical current, a snap of lightning, flowed between them. Even when they were a few feet apart, it seemed as if they touched.

He unfolded himself and straightened. He embraced the tranquility he felt when he was with her, and their evening had passed in a blur of laughs and kisses and a hint of rose-wood perfume from her fragrant hair.

Peace was indeed a part of her, a serenity and contentment he attributed to more than her excitement for the upcoming Christmas season. It was her Christian faith. This woman, this town, was a shift for him, when his daily life was filled with more duties than he could accomplish.

He mentioned as much to Gerry when they met a few days later for an impromptu jam session at Musically Yours. Dorothy had afforded them an after-hours studio, and the men had gratefully accepted.

A grin on his weather-beaten features, his fuzzy eyebrows raised in a tickled question, Gerry responded by saying, "So, you're in love?"

Max pulled back, disconcerted. "Who said that?"

"You did."

"When?"

"By your eyes, words and actions."

Max navigated to safer ground. "You sure you don't mind

meeting here to rehearse? The drive from Perrytown is a haul for you."

"You and I share a passion for music, and rehearsing in person is a blessing."

Max tugged out his harmonica. "I assume your wife is understanding about the hours away from little Freddie?"

"Totally. As long as I'm home by ten o'clock." Gerry set an amp on the floor, then searched for an outlet. He plugged one end of a cable into the amp, the other into the guitar. Snaps and shrill bangs followed, and Gerry switched the volume down.

Because Max lived a few blocks from the store, he had walked, admiring the decorations on the way over, likening them to a Christmas postcard.

The temperature had dropped in the past few days, and blades of grass peeked through a frost of white. Holly bushes were in vibrant red-berry bloom, and blinking red, green, and white lights were everywhere.

He passed a busy coffee shop with folks bustling in and emerging with large cups of hot chocolate topped with creamy whipped cream. Aromas of fresh brewed coffee and toasty chocolate brought scents of the season to mind. A vendor on the corner peddled roasted chestnuts in paper cones. Giggling youngsters ran by him, their laughter high-spirited over the chatter of adults. On side streets, flickering candles gleamed from residences, and vibrant lights from their evergreen trees shone from the windows.

Max never remembered decorating a pine tree, except for the year with Lenny and his family. The snapshot of that one perfect tree, the one perfect Christmas, lived forever in his mind.

When he reached Musically Yours, he was immediately immersed in the harmonies of guitar music sounding from the speakers, the cozy overhead lights, and the warmth of an excellent heating system. After greeting Gerry, who was already there, he asked what they were listening to.

"Joseph Slater's newest worship song, a contemporary Christian arrangement," Gerry noted. "He slowed the tempo, kept the instrumentals simple, and let his voice do the heavy lifting. He's an awesome vocalist."

"Awesome, indeed." Max tilted his head, and allowed the poignant lyrics to wash over him.

"'Mary Did You Know?' is one of my favorite pieces," Gerry said. "Are you aware that the composer took seven years to complete it?"

"Good things are worth the wait, time, and effort," Max replied. "And when you find something good?"

"Never let her go."

Max regarded Gerry. "I'm assuming you mean Sarah?" he asked, and then went on to talk about her in such a way that Gerry told him he was in love.

Gerry brought on a grin and didn't reply.

Focus on the music, Max told himself as Gerry finished tuning his guitar.

They decided on a playlist for their upcoming performance—a medley of carols that included, "O Christmas Tree," "Santa Claus Is Coming To Town," and the finale, "The Twelve Days of Christmas."

"A fun holiday singalong," Gerry said. "For the encore, we'll perform "All Is Well," which is uplifting and inspirational."

"You're certain we'll get enough applause for an encore?"

"Stranger things have happened," Gerry mused while he plucked his guitar. "On another note, my wife and baby are attending. My mother-in-law too."

"How's little Freddie lately?"

"I anticipate my wife's hasty exit after our first song."

"Hopefully, we won't sound that bad."

"We're fairly decent. Besides, my wife deserves a night out."

"With little Freddie," Max reminded with a grin. He pointed to an autographed album hanging on a wall, the cover depicting Joseph Slater and an acoustic guitar. "Musically Yours sure promotes this guy."

"He's a big-name artist who lives in Cherish."

"Joseph settled here," Max mused, arching a single eyebrow.

"Same goes for Ryan Edwards. Love is like a fairy-tale, at least that's what my wife parrots. Joseph met Scarlett when he was here for a music promotion. He decided to put down roots after all those years of touring and married her last year."

"Because of Scarlett, he gave up his career?"

"Hardly. Life is a compromise, my friend, and you're clearly smitten too. Are you still coming to my house on Christmas Day for dinner?"

"Unless you're having second thoughts."

"On the contrary, I'm thinking about inviting my great-niece to join us."

Max beamed. "A tremendous idea."

"I suspected you'd be receptive." Gerry smirked, then leaned back in a wooden chair he'd snagged from the student waiting area. "Now let's rock-and-roll to some favorite Christmas carols."

*O*n the Friday evening of The Bearded Elves' debut, Sarah grabbed a seat at a round table near the band, along with Dorothy, Ryan, Gerry's wife and son and mother-in-law, Nicholas, and Emmanuelle.

She'd dressed with care for the evening—a fit and flare lace dress, strappy leopard print heels she already wanted to kick off, and sparkly gumdrop-red earrings. She'd topped her outfit with the fine royal blue wool coat she wore on special occasions.

During the past two weeks, lighthearted conversations and dinners with Max at The Garden Terrace, their stolen kisses, their bantering texts, had become routine. Max invited her on another hike, and she'd happily accepted.

Each time they parted, he promised to see or text her the following day.

And he always did.

She should have been joyful. She was. But a heaviness weighed on her spirit because the days flew too quickly. Soon, January would arrive.

Refreshed by endless glasses of sugar-free lemonade, she sang along to the familiar carols with the others, especially during Ryan's sidesplitting rendition of "The Twelve Days Of Christmas."

As he reached the final, "And a partridge in a pear tree," his operatic voice swelled through the restaurant.

Max confirmed his ability as an excellent harmonica player. He'd been too modest, she thought. Whenever he hit an imagined wrong note, he glanced at her with a chagrined smile. The keen, honed bite of blues he produced on such an inexpensive instrument proved him a man of many talents, and pride flowed through her.

Can you believe the tunes a person can produce from such a modest instrument? he had texted a few days earlier. *Wood, two pieces of metal and minute brass reeds.*

The only thing I can play is the radio, she'd texted back in jest, despite his assurances that he would teach her how to read music.

When? she'd wanted to ask. However, she remained silent.

Wait till you hear our encore, he'd responded.

What's the name of the song?

It's an inspirational piece. It'll bring tears to your eyes.

She was seeing a side of him she hadn't envisioned beneath his polka-dotted bow tie, chambray shirt, and jeans —a look she'd catalogued as distinctly Max.

During each fifteen-minute break between sets, he'd made it a point to sit next to her. He drew her close, his arm draped around her shoulders in a gesture that seemed possessive, but delighted Sarah immeasurably.

After the band's first set, Melissa, the baby, and her mother left. Little Freddie had been fairly well-behaved, and Melissa and her mother had taken turns walking around the restaurant to soothe the baby.

Sarah surprised herself by offering to help. She'd never been an active participant in group situations, and had felt increasingly uncomfortable in even small crowds now—reticent to speak in case she'd misheard someone, and hesitant to ask people to repeat themselves.

In any case, she wasn't used to these feelings—the attention from Max, the joy of being among a welcoming, friendly group. This was camaraderie, sharing jubilant hours with friends and family who cared.

After the rousing rendition of "The Twelve Days of Christmas," Gerry and Max grinned and bowed to enthusiastic applause. As calls for an encore rose, Max stepped down from the small stage. Dorothy stopped him, saying something to him. Sarah couldn't see Dorothy's face, but she could see Max's, and she couldn't resist eavesdropping by reading his lips.

"January first," he seemed to be saying, "I'm eager to leave for Florida and head up an ornithology department."

January. Leave. Eager.

Sarah's stomach tightened.

She half rose in her seat. But no, she shouldn't be

surprised. He'd repeatedly cited his new Jacksonville job. His time in Cherish was temporary.

Unexpectedly weak, she braced her hands on the arms of her chair. She'd been a fool for falling for him. Hoping against hope, while knowing the romance would come to an end in January.

Questions surfaced with no answers. He was a man of his word and had accepted the university position months ago.

Nevertheless, confronting the pain of his departure brought unexpected heartache. They'd never actually discussed him leaving. It was a point in the future neither had chosen to broach.

No matter. She'd slip into the background again, a pattern she'd honed over the years. Loneliness encroached so swiftly she couldn't react, save for tugging on her shoes and scouting out the quickest path to the exit.

She'd been unmoored by the attentions of a stranger. She'd only known him a few weeks. *A few enchanted weeks.*

She swallowed hard and stood to leave as soon as Max and Gerry returned to the stage to more applause. The diners had awarded the men a standing ovation, and the enthusiastic applause soon quieted.

Max angled a glance at her with a broad smile. *Success*, he seemed to say. *Thank you for supporting me and my music.*

She grabbed her coat and turned away, then rounded to glimpse him one last time. His chin drew in, perplexed, as he lifted the harmonica to his lips.

Dorothy caught her hand. "You're leaving? What about the last song?"

"It's later than I thought." Sarah made a show of peering at her watch, aware of how quiet everyone at her table had become. However, she couldn't face another conversation with Max.

From the onset, he'd spoken the truth. Nonetheless, truth

was difficult to confront, especially when it waylaid you at the happiest moment of your life.

Nicholas stood and excused himself from the others. "Sarah, I'll walk you to the door."

"Thanks. I can manage." She veered left, away from him, struggling to keep her emotions in check.

"It's no bother. I have an ulterior motive."

They passed straggling diners, plates of food being cleared from empty tables by tired-looking waitresses, while Max's bluesy harmonica accompanied Gerry's vocals.

"'All is well all is well, ... Sing Alleluia.'"

"It'll bring tears to your eyes," Max had said.

And it did.

The lyrics were hopeful and encouraging, and Max harmonized with Gerry, his baritone voice complementing the uplifting words.

A Christian song. Max was singing a Christian song.

"What's your motive?" she asked Nicholas when they reached the entry. "The abandoned puppy?"

"Yep. And if I don't find a home for him, he'll end up in an animal shelter. It's a no-kill shelter, but still ..." His words trailed off.

She opened her mouth. Closed it. She was about to refuse when she paused. A darling puppy would be the ideal distraction for her hurt heart.

"I'll take him," she burst out.

"Sarah, thank you! Why did you change your mind?"

"I can't let a lovable puppy spend the holidays in a shelter."

"I'll bring him over to your house in a couple days." Clearly, Nicholas was uncertain whether he'd understood her. "I realize Christmas Eve is almost here ..."

"No worries. The puppy has spent too many nights alone already."

CHAPTER TEN

*O*n Christmas Eve, Sarah sat alone.

Only for tonight. Tomorrow, she would drive to Perrytown to dine with her great-uncle, his wife, and little Freddie. He'd phoned her, and she'd gratefully accepted the invitation. In years past, she'd spent Christmas Day with her parents and brothers, traveling to their homes in the Carolina mountains. They'd moved away from Cherish, and she was the only one who had remained.

This year, she'd elected to stay home with her growing number of animals.

She had already attended the three o'clock church service. She'd done so purposely, in order not to run into Max, who would be singing in the choir at the six o'clock service. Right about now, he would be entering the church to get ready.

She'd returned from the service invigorated and encouraged. The sermon had touched on how God didn't free people from traumatic situations, but rather, He was there walking with them every step of the way.

Yes, she'd experienced troubles and challenges. However, any expectations fixed on the Messiah to grant a person's peace came from within. God didn't promise an easy life, and Sarah couldn't experience peace when she had been anticipating a textbook Christmas with the man she loved.

Her mind traveled back to the loving way Max had regarded her—by the river, at the restaurant, in his home. His tenderness when he kissed her.

No. She couldn't allow him into her thoughts anymore. He belonged to the huge, widespread world of birds and his research, not the microscopic town of Cherish.

Yet she'd felt loved and protected when his lips pressed against hers—his strong arms shielding her when they'd encountered that bear.

She hadn't wanted to lose that, the sense of being cherished and safeguarded.

But Max's love was never hers to begin with.

She peered at the roly-poly puppy nestled in his crate. Already, he'd created a wealth of joy in a short period of time.

He was beginning to eat solids, and she'd continued the transition of soaking the food in warm water, then blending it to the texture of gruel. A fresh supply of water was ever present.

The past couple days, she'd brought his toys into her home first for the other animals to sniff. When the puppy arrived, the dogs ignored him except for an occasional sniff. She'd rewarded their unaggressive behavior with upbeat praise, and had placed the resident dogs' toys and food bowls in a separate location.

Likewise, the cats wandered over for a sniff, then dismissed the puppy.

Sarah's goal was to allow the animals to learn to trust each other. So far, so good.

She switched on a holiday radio station, and The Mormon Tabernacle choir sang "Adeste Fideles" in Latin.

Max would've appreciated the arrangement. He was so musical.

Sighing, she looked at the framed photo on her side table. When she had finally scrolled through the photos she'd taken with her cell phone the day of their hike, she found a wonderful one of Max. It was a profile picture. His face had been near the camera, and every handsome quality was evident—the dark stubble of his beard, his silver-gray eyes, his determined demeanor.

She'd also gotten a surprisingly good photo of the bear. She'd auto-merged them into a silly collage, the bear and Max staring at each other, eye to eye.

She'd planned to gift him the photo and had bought a wooden frame depicting the great outdoors with the words Into the Woods on it. She'd captioned the photo, "I knew we were safe all along."

Max's words.

She would never hear his voice again. She squeezed her eyes shut and took a deep breath. "I love you, Max," she murmured, vowing to rely on time and faith to heal her broken heart.

She slid the photo into a bag and placed it in a drawer in the side table.

*a*s Max looked around the church on Christmas Eve from his vantage point on the top riser, his heart dropped. He scanned the pews—the exquisitely appointed windows and the altar bedecked with the brilliant display of flowers that Sarah had arranged. But Sarah was not there.

"Surely, she'll attend church," he muttered to Gerry, as the men took their places in the baritone section.

Marge Addyson, standing near the altar, turned. "She attended the earlier service," she said.

She did? Why?

Two days ago, Sarah had left The Garden Terrace before The Bearded Elves' performance was over and without a farewell. Thereafter, Max's phone calls and voice mails had gone unanswered.

The previous morning, he'd stopped by the nursery. Her coworker, Bonnie, declared that Sarah was in the greenhouse dealing with seedlings and couldn't be disturbed.

The service ended with the cantata and Max's harmonica solo. When the service was over, he exited the church with his heart touched and his spirits lifted. The sermon had delivered a message of optimistic goodwill.

"God's son appeared in the least likely situation and to humble people," the pastor had addressed the congregation. "Forgive and let your resentments go. What will prevent your happiness is to strive for perfection in yourself and others."

Hadn't Max always sought excellence? Blame it on his upbringing, but he'd endeavored to become top-notch in his profession. But what good was that perfection without someone to love?

Unwilling to accept the end of their relationship, he strode from the church to Sarah's house. In a short time, he'd become accustomed to small-town living, where most places were within a few blocks' walking distance. He'd purchased a special present for her and held the package securely under his arm.

When he reached her house, he stood silently on her front porch. Although he didn't move, wild barking sounded from inside before he could even knock.

Then the barking ceased.

He knocked, hesitant to ring her doorbell. Okay, maybe he shouldn't have dropped by unannounced, but what else could he do when she kept slipping away from him?

Suppose she was sleeping?

At eight o'clock on a clear and cold Christmas Eve? Sarah? Unless she wasn't home ... But where ...

Tiny yelps sounded. A yipping.

The door opened a crack, and a wobbly puppy shoved his nose through the opening, wagging a fluffy white tail.

Sarah scooped up the puppy, then gasped as she stood in the doorway. "Max?"

"Merry Christmas."

"How long were you standing on the porch?"

He shrugged. "A while."

"What were you doing?"

"Praying."

"Praying? What are you praying for? An extraordinary gift on Christmas Eve?"

"I'm praying for the most extraordinary of gifts. You."

Her striking green eyes glistened with tears, her features a flood of emotions. "Merry Christmas."

"May I come in?" She couldn't just stand at the door holding a puppy.

"Yes. Please."

He stepped inside and brushed a kiss across her temple. She cuddled the tiny Yorkipoo to her chest. He grinned at the pom-pom tail, the paws reminding him of a hedgehog, and the molten-brown eyes peeking beneath half-closed lids. Perhaps he wasn't a Yorkipoo ...

"Apparently, Sheriff Nicholas convinced you?" Max asked as he stroked the puppy's velvety fur.

"Careful," she warned. "His teeth are like little needles." She set the puppy inside a blanketed crate. The two older dogs settled. The cats walked away.

And Sarah walked into Max's embrace.

He drew her closer, pressing his lips to hers, fearful to break the hold for fear she might disappear.

When the kiss ended, she rubbed her cheek against his jacket. "I'm glad you're here."

Her home wasn't decorated for the holidays, which surprised him, considering her festive porch.

"My fake tree and ornaments are in the attic." She seemed to read his mind. "I haven't had time."

Or rather, had she felt like him, and didn't have the heart to decorate?

She was gorgeous in a crimson cashmere sweater and form-fitting black pants. Her figure was trim with curves, a wreath of dark russet curls framed her perfect face.

"I do have appropriate holiday cookies and eggnog, if you're interested," she said. "And both were bought from the grocery store."

They shared another commonality besides coffee and hiking and a love for animals. They appreciated store-bought items when homemade wasn't an option. Or, he supposed, even if it was.

He smiled, removed his jacket, and adjusted his bow tie. For the Christmas Eve service, he'd elected to wear black dress pants and a crisp white shirt.

"Can I be direct?" he asked, after she'd taken a jug out of the refrigerator, poured him a glass of eggnog, and set out a platter of frosted vanilla sugar cookies in the shape of snowmen.

"I wouldn't expect anything else."

He placed his gift on the coffee table. He'd wrapped it in plain brown paper tied with twine, topped with a green and white parakeet ornament.

"Why did you leave the restaurant without saying good-bye?" His hand slid up her arm in a caress. "Furthermore, why were you avoiding me? Is my singing that bad?"

She smiled. "No."

"I'd like to continue seeing you."

She fixed her gaze on a point beyond him. "I can't deal with a long-distance relationship and you're leaving for Jacksonville in a week."

He heard the hurt in her tone. His gaze stayed on her.

He invited her to sit on the sofa in the living room and he settled beside her. "Who said I was moving to Jacksonville?"

"You've mentioned little else since you arrived in Cherish. The other night at The Garden Terrace when you spoke with Dorothy, you declared your eagerness to leave for Florida in January and head an ornithology department."

And then it hit him. Sarah cared about him. Deeply. So deeply, she couldn't face him leaving.

And he was delighted.

He pulled her nearer. "I said I was eager to greet the new head of the ornithology department in Florida in January."

She blinked. "I don't understand."

"I declined the position. The latest candidate is a colleague from my New York university days who's done amazing research on zebra finches. She's a workaholic and will be an excellent fit."

"So much for my lip-reading abilities. And eavesdropping." Sarah sat straighter. "You didn't accept the position?"

"No."

"I made an appointment with an audiologist to test my hearing. I've read that I won't be as fatigued at the end of the day if I haven't had to struggle with the effort of listening."

"If you indeed have a hearing loss, it should be addressed." Max smoothed his lips over her hair. "I should've been clearer about my feelings. I would've been if you hadn't vanished."

"I haven't gone anywhere."

"This project has involved numerous researchers working around the world. My bit with budgies is only a small part of the larger study on birdsongs."

"And?"

"The paper will take a couple years to complete, especially as current research sends scientists in different directions. Which means I'm not going anywhere. I can continue my research here and will receive a full-time salary."

"You're staying in Cherish?"

"I renewed my lease on 8 Poplar Lane."

"Does this mean more hiking adventures?"

"Weekly." He grinned. "This place, and you, have allowed me to slow down and reflect. However, I will have to travel to Jacksonville twice a semester to meet with other members of the department. I'm hoping you'll accompany me."

"I'd love to."

"I'd also like to visit the university I attended in New York."

"I've never seen a big city."

"New York is filled with diversity, culture, and excitement. I'll take you to see the famous landmarks."

"I'd like that," she said softly.

"And I have a brother in Portugal."

"Yes."

"I need to reach out to him again. If he invites us to travel to Portugal to visit him, will you accompany me?"

She nodded. "Happily."

"Good." He peered upward. "Where's your attic?"

"You're looking in the right direction."

"I've only decorated a Christmas tree once in my life—with Lenny and his family."

"Is that a hint?"

"A broad hint. But first." He nodded to his gift.

Glancing at him, she unraveled the twine. In the box was an ornament—a bear, hiker boots and the inscription, "Take a hike."

She smiled, smoothed her fingers over the words, then curled near him. "You remembered?"

"Of course. After numerous phone requests to the ranger, a shipment finally arrived."

"Thank you." She slid open a drawer in the table beside her and handed him a bag. "I'm sorry it isn't wrapped. By the time the order arrived, I assumed I'd never see you again."

"Yet here I am." He pulled the frame out of the bag and read aloud her caption. "I knew we were safe all along."

"Because we'll do life together."

For a long while, he held her. "I missed you at church tonight. Mrs. Addyson remarked on the preacher's outstanding sermon."

"Yes. I thought so too."

"I played the harmonica. The choir was beautiful."

"I'm sure they were. I'm sure you were awesome."

"You'll hear me play and sing again because I joined the choir." He tipped back his head, as if he were gazing toward heaven. "I was distracted—by my bitterness, and by life. I'm starting to realize that God is for me, not against me. My perspective was messed up, but finally, at forty, I'm seeing more clearly."

"God has always been your champion. He is never against you."

She whispered a word of praise, and Max joined in.

"Gerry declared that dinner tomorrow is at two o'clock, give or take a few hours," she said.

He returned her smile. "He told me the same. I guess it depends on little Freddie's schedule."

She hesitated. "I didn't realize you were dining there too."

"He didn't mention it?" Max chuckled. "He must've forgotten when he phoned you."

"You knew he called?"

"I stood next to him when he made the phone call."

"So, you figured between tonight and tomorrow, we'd see each other?"

"That's one of the things I love about Christmas. All this togetherness." He reached for his jacket and pulled out a handful of wildflowers from his pocket—intense violets and pale blue ivy. "These grow at the edge of town. I'm impressed that plants bloom here in the winter. I'd forgotten. In any event, I picked them for you. Sorry they're wilted."

"They're not. They're beautiful."

He muffled her protest with a deep kiss and drew her into his arms. "I can't give you much, but I'll give you my love."

"I love you too."

The puppy whimpered, and Sarah freed him from his crate and nestled him in her arms. When Max extended his hands, she placed the tiny bundle in his lap.

"What's his name?" he asked.

"Tiny Tim."

Max swallowed the thickness in his throat, the emotions overcoming him.

He drew Sarah near. She was all he needed, all he'd been searching for. The woman he loved by his side, a reverence for a God who was no longer elusive, and a significant, heart-warming Christmas.

"Merry Christmas, Max," Sarah whispered. "And God bless us, every one."

. . .

The End

A NOTE FROM JOSIE

Dear Friend,

Thank you for reading my holiday romance, A Christmas Puppy To Cherish. I hope you enjoyed this heartwarming, inspirational story. This is the fourth book in my contemporary "Cherish" series.

You don't need ears to hear God's plan. All you need is an open heart...

This story is set in the charming fictional small town of Cherish, South Carolina. The book follows A Love Song To Cherish, A Christmas To Cherish, and A Valentine To Cherish.

In A Christmas Puppy To Cherish, I introduce two new characters to our beloved mix of familiar heroes and heroines. Many of you may know that music is an important part of my life, and many of the characters are musicians.

I also researched the hero, Maxwell's, fascinating profession of ornithology. (The study of birds.)

And the heroine, Sarah, with her kind heart, is the perfect match for him.

The 5th book in the Cherish series is A Homecoming To Cherish, featuring a single mother struggling to raise her teenage daughter.

The final book is A Summer To Cherish, featuring a despondent artist losing his vision, and the spunky, independent woman who encourages him.

If you loved this story as much as I loved writing it, please help other people find it by posting your review.

A Christmas Puppy To Cherish is available in ebook, Paperback, Hardcover, and Large Print Paperback. Also available in Audiobook.

I'd love to meet you in person someday, but in the meantime, all I can offer is a sincere and grateful thank you. Without your support, my books would not be possible.

As I write my next sweet or inspirational romance, remember this: Have you ever tried something you were afraid to try because it mattered so much to you? I did, when I started writing. Take the chance, and just do something you love.

With sincere appreciation,

Josie Riviera

My Spotify List for A Christmas Puppy To Cherish is here.

Love sweet and wholesome holiday romances? Check out these boxed sets:

Holiday Hearts Book Bundle Volume One
Holiday Hearts Book Bundle Volume Two
Holiday Hearts Book Bundle Volume Three
Holiday Hearts Book Bundle Volume Four
Holiday Hearts Book Bundle Volume Five

Want more of the inspirational Cherish series?

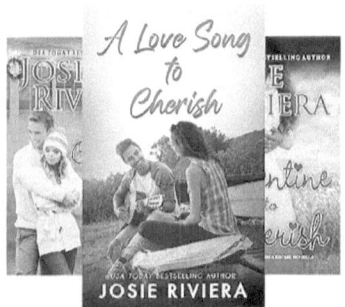

Or grab Cherished Hearts.

The entire series! 6 sweet, inspirational romances in 1 giant boxed set.

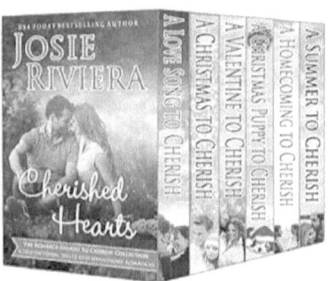

AMANDA'S EASY WASSAIL

Ingredients:

2 cups apple juice
    2 cups orange juice
    2 cups cranberry juice
    2 cinnamon sticks

Add everything to a crockpot, mix, and warm until the desired temperature is reached.

For a larger batch: (almost a gallon)

5 cups apple juice
    5 cups orange juice
    5 cups cranberry juice
    3 or 4 cinnamon sticks, as desired

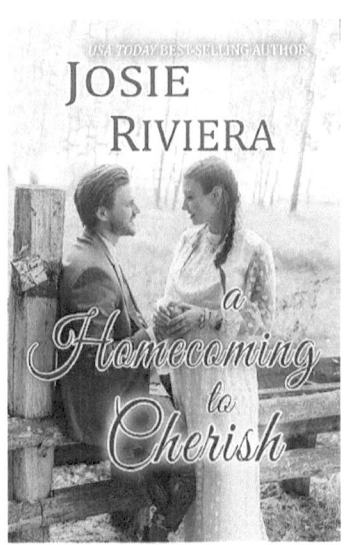

CHAPTER ONE

"You expect us to live here, in this stuffy little town with one traffic light?" Samantha, Nora Lancaster's fifteen-year-old daughter, stood on the steps of the Cherish Hills Inn, arms crossed, wearing her infamous, *I'm bored*, pout. The hot-pink beanie that she wore no matter the weather, sat askew on her head, a whimsical contrast to her black curly hair.

"Why? What's wrong with Cherish?" With an encouraging smile, Nora surveyed the inn. "Wow. The exterior is still painted white."

"Actually, the paint is peeling, Mom, though I wasn't talking about the inn. I was referring to the town."

"We're only here for a month," Nora replied.

"An entire month without seeing my boyfriend! Four whole weeks."

"What's his name again? Eric?"

"Edison."

"I can't keep track. Your boyfriends change regularly."

"Edison is awesome."

"Edison. Like the lightbulb?"

"Yeah, Mom, he's a lightbulb." Samantha breezed past her mother's comment. "He's the cutest boy in the senior class, and his parents are allowing him to drive to Cherish so we can study together. They're buying him a car for his eighteenth birthday."

"Because he invented the lightbulb?"

"Not funny, Mom." Nora had learned to ignore her daughter's eye rolls, though it was still difficult. "I'll turn sixteen soon, and then I'll be able to get my license too."

"Whoa. Backpedal. Study for what? You completed your school term early."

Samantha and a boy alone in a car, plus the idea of Samantha driving set off heart palpitations.

However, Nora had felt the same way when she was only a few years older than Samantha was now. She'd wanted her independence. Once she became a teen, she'd counted the days until she could hightail it out of Cherish. Lifting heavy linens, changing beds in the inn's guestrooms, and fatigue had taken its toll. Along with school, no opportunity remained for fun, extracurricular activities.

She'd appreciated the supportive encouragement from her parents, and the camaraderie with the inn's handful of workers had resulted in friendships. However, at the end of the day, friendship hadn't been enough. Nora had slaved at the inn all those hours ... for what? An inn repeatedly on the brink of bankruptcy?

Luckily, she'd never been a boy-crazy teenager.

Or had she?

Nora's gaze strayed to Samantha's precocious smile, and her heart swelled. Oversized hoop earrings and a silver-studded belt were expressions of Samantha's personality, but didn't take away from her fresh-faced beauty. People remarked that mother and daughter were mirror images, although Samantha was slim, whereas Nora carried twenty extra pounds on her five-foot-eight-inch frame.

"This little town isn't how I remembered." She grinned at her fond childhood memories—skipping in the park, playing hopscotch with friends after school, and eating Dutch chocolate ice cream at the local ice cream parlor.

Truth be told, her younger days had been filled with happiness. This self-contained community of Cherish, which she'd termed claustrophobic once she hit her teens, embraced respectability and decency. What was wrong with that?

However, to sustain the anger toward her parents, Nora had zeroed in on the disagreeable moments. She'd shut the door on the pleasant times and locked her heart, simpler than confronting her weariness and frustration.

"How do you remember the town?" Samantha seemed suddenly talkative.

"Short-sighted." Nora searched for a better answer, though none came.

"Which was what, thirty years ago, Mom?"

"More like fifteen, honey. I'm not that ancient." Nora pinned on a smile, grabbed Samantha's hand, and mounted the expansive porch stairs to the front door of the inn. As expected, Samantha tugged free from her grip.

I could use some help with this young woman, Nora thought. Similar to most teens, Samantha wanted to fit in while asserting her individuality. On a good day, Nora glimpsed her daughter's former sweet self, though she'd quickly close up, perhaps for fear of sharing too much. An image of a giggling, pudgy-cheeked toddler surfaced. Where had her pleasant little girl gone?

"Look at it this way." Nora kept her smile. "You completed the semester early, so now you'll enjoy a longer summer recess."

"Enjoy? Here? I didn't mind getting out of dull, boring school, but living in Cherish for a month isn't a vacation."

"I didn't say it was. I suggested it was an opportunity." Nora turned to take in the picturesque street—the rows of flowering trees, the orange daylilies lining the sidewalk, the cheerful *Good mornings* from folks passing by. Why hadn't she appreciated the joy of ordinary life in this quaint town? Lately, her accounting job in Richmond had carried more and more responsibility and later evenings.

It was wrong, she knew it was wrong, to agree to overtime instead of spending the evenings with her daughter. Even so, Nora was the lone parent who paid the bills.

"An opportunity to work with no salary?" Samantha challenged her.

"Volunteer work is the best kind." Nora turned to her daughter. "Besides, where else would you rather be?"

"Back home in Virginia." A frown from Samantha. "Or sunny Florida, or an exotic island in the Pacific."

"I'll keep it in mind," Nora replied with a teasing laugh.

They both knew that wouldn't happen. Nora was fortunate to have an excellent paying job, a lucrative career. Nevertheless, she still struggled financially.

The door of the inn opened, revealing a skinny, elderly man with stark-white hair. A scowl took over his vein-reddened features.

Nora shouldered her purse and came forward. "Hi. Mr. Canning?"

He shoved up his cheater eyeglasses. "Call me Tom."

Scarcely the greeting Nora had hoped for. Her shoulder muscles tightened as she approached. "Hello, Tom. I'm Nora Lancaster. We spoke several times on the phone." She twisted, revealing her daughter standing behind her. "And this is Samantha."

"Hi." Samantha gave a half-hearted wave.

"I figured." Tom rolled up the sleeves of his tan-colored shirt, exposing thin, pointy elbows. "You're the woman who wants to take my inn away from me."

"Hardly," Nora said. "I'm ... I mean *we're* here to help with any work required around the inn until you're fully recovered."

She didn't dare make eye contact with her daughter, assuming Samantha's over-tweezed eyebrows were raised. Lately, the words *help* and *work* weren't in her daughter's vocabulary.

"I'm standing here," Tom was saying. "I am recovered, and I told you not to come."

"And I told you I was coming, regardless. Heart attacks require rest and recuperation, and you spent only three days in the hospital."

"Are you spying on me?"

"On the contrary, I'm concerned."

He scowled. "Nowadays, hospitals don't keep patients any longer than necessary."

"True." Nora regarded his pale features, the stoop of his

shoulders. "Nonetheless, you can neither rest nor recuperate if you're operating this place by yourself."

"My employee, Louise, has been with me a decade," Tom replied. "I can't run the inn without her."

"I'm certain she's a hard worker, notwithstanding the fact that your large inn requires more help."

"Are you a doctor?"

"I'm an accountant." Nora shifted. "However, I can visualize every corner of the inn because I worked here nonstop when I was younger. I'm also familiar with the community mindset, and from what I've observed so far, nothing has changed."

"Precisely how the townsfolk like it."

"I remember when my parents wrote to tell me they'd sold the inn to you. I want to make certain you don't lose it as they did."

The warm June air stilled. Nora chastised herself for speaking her fears aloud.

"Are you saying I'm not capable of running my own inn?" Tom asked. "I bought this place from them, fair and square."

Nora breathed in. She should be patient and tactful. She had had enough conversations with Tom to know he was hard on himself for not being able to do what he used to in his younger days.

"My offer comes with no obligation," she said. "You know, it's okay to accept help from someone who cares."

He raised his milk-white eyebrows at Samantha. "There won't be much for a young person to do."

Samantha grunted her assent.

"She's ambitious," Nora put in. "She's able."

"Right." His tone reflected precisely the opposite. "Decades have passed. Doesn't mean you have a legal claim to the inn now."

"I never suggested that."

He blew out a loud breath. "I was surprised when you contacted me."

"I understand. I've simply kept an eye on it all these years."

"Why?"

"Because it was a part of my every waking hour while I was growing up. Besides ..."

She shifted.

Nope. Not going there. Some subjects were too personal. Guilt rose—brought on by the urgency to fix what she'd come to regret.

He inspected her from head to toe. "I don't remember the likes of you when I bought the place."

"I'd left by then." She curled her fingers around the strap of her handbag. "Moved out of town and got married."

"Your parents were nice people."

Were being the operative word.

She swallowed. "They died in a car accident not long after they sold the inn to you."

"I'm sorry."

"Me too."

"Where's your husband?" He peered here and there, as if a husband might miraculously appear.

"We've been divorced for many years." Nora shoved past the troublesome thoughts whenever a conversation alluded to her ex. Samantha didn't seem to care that she'd never known her father. He'd left when she was an infant.

"Uh, huh," Tom said.

Somehow, Nora felt like her lack of a partner was a strike against her.

Please Lord, don't let Tom turn me aside.

Why was a prayer coming to mind? She'd avoided religion for years.

"I ... we can pretty much handle any chores and duties."

Nora concentrated on Tom. "My accounting background and experience can't hurt either."

"I'll admit your timing is excellent." He closed his mouth, then opened it again. "Mondays are slow, and only a few guests are here."

She patted her daughter's shoulder. "We're ready to assist and can start immediately."

"Tomorrow, eight more guests are arriving." Tom tilted his head to the side. "Three are an advance team from Fresh 'n' Good, a high-end chain that might open a new restaurant in town."

"I've heard of them. One of their restaurants is near us in Virginia."

"Probably several." Tom snorted. "One guy from the chain has already arrived."

"You offer dining here too. I saw that on your website, clicked on all the photos."

"I should update the website." Tom scratched his head. "I usually rely on one of the busboys to do it. Teenagers can do these things in a snap."

Nora nodded. "Nowadays, guests expect up-to-date information." She didn't add that the website was outdated.

"My restaurant has been a success up till now," Tom went on. "We're little, though, and Fresh 'n' Good is big." He tugged on the hem of his crewneck sweater. "C'mon inside. Photos are fine, but showing you the inn is better. Besides, I ought to sit down."

"Our luggage is in my car."

"No one will steal it. I figured you were hard-headed and would come anyway, so I asked Louise to prepare rooms for you upstairs."

Nora and Samantha followed him through the carpeted hallway to an expansive parlor, and the fragrant traces of flowers filled the space. A glass vase of crimson roses was set on a cherry wood table, and sunlight gleamed through the front window. Defining the seating area, a cornflower-blue tapestry rug covered a portion of the oak wood floor.

He waited while Nora and Samantha settled on an over-stuffed sofa. With a slight groan, he sagged into the chair across from them. Life-sized ceramic roosters faced each other on the mantel of the stacked rock fireplace.

The interior was a bit dusty and messy, and countless knickknacks added a colonial-flavored clutter to the space. In fact, both the interior and exterior screamed for a thorough cleaning and update. Old-fashioned dark paneling covered two walls, and the plaid patterned wallpaper on the other ones created a folksy flavor that might not appeal to the current market.

Nora folded her hands on her lap. "Will the new restaurant threaten the livelihood of existing local eateries like yours?"

"Maybe. Maybe not. We pride ourselves on our signature desserts, all prepared in house." He hesitated, though not for long. "You mentioned you could begin immediately."

"Immediately?" Samantha, who had been busy scrolling through her cellphone, came to full attention.

Tom stared out the window, away from them. "The doctor advised me not to do anything too physical this month," he mumbled.

"Sound advice." Nora stood. "We'll grab our luggage, freshen up, and start in an hour."

She ignored the gasp from her daughter. Instead, she signaled Samantha to follow her to the car to help carry the luggage.

*** End of Excerpt: A Homecoming to Cherish by Josie Riviera ***

Keep reading on Amazon. FREE on Kindle Unlimited.

ABOUT THE AUTHOR

Josie Riviera is a *USA TODAY* bestselling author of contemporary, inspirational, and historical sweet romances that read like Hallmark movies. She lives in the Charlotte, NC, area with her wonderfully supportive husband. They share their home with an adorable shih tzu, who constantly needs grooming, and live in an old house forever needing renovations.

To receive my Newsletter and your free sweet romance novella ebook as a thank you gift, sign up HERE.

Become a member of my Read and Review VIP Facebook group for exclusive giveaways and ARCs.

josieriviera.com

ACKNOWLEDGMENTS

An appreciative thank you to my patient husband, Dave, and our three wonderful children.

ALSO BY JOSIE RIVIERA

Seeking Patience

Seeking Catherine (always Free!)

Seeking Fortune

Seeking Charity

Seeking Rachel

The Seeking Series

Oh Danny Boy

I Love You More

A Snowy White Christmas

A Portuguese Christmas

Holiday Hearts Book Bundle Volume One

Holiday Hearts Book Bundle Volume Two

Holiday Hearts Book Bundle Volume Three

Holiday Hearts Book Bundle Volume Four

Holiday Hearts Book Bundle Volume Five

Candleglow and Mistletoe

Maeve (Perfect Match)

A Christmas To Cherish

A Love Song To Cherish

A Valentine To Cherish

A Christmas Puppy To Cherish

A Homecoming To Cherish

Romance Stories To Cherish

Aloha to Love

A Very Christian Christmas

The 1-800-Series Volume Two

The 1-800-Series Complete

Christmas Tails of the Heart

Cocoa's Christmas Love

Pawfect Christmas Hearts

Pink Coral Island

Most books are available in ebook, audiobook, paperback, Large Print paperback and Hardcover.

Many are FREE on Kindle Unlimited!